Damaged Daddy

An Age Gap Off-Limits Romance

By

Pebble James

Prologue

Five months earlier...

Randall Donovan sat in the corner of the viewing room at the Murphy Funeral Home, wondering how his life had come to this moment. Just one week ago, Rand was out in their backyard bar-be-queuing hamburgers for his family and a few friends located in the same cul-de-sac. Five days ago, he was walking through the front door after a long day at the community college where he was in his ninth year of teaching 19th Century Poetry. Three days ago, he was at the college late grading mid-final papers and supposed to be getting ready to meet his wife, Marie, at their favorite restaurant for an anniversary dinner.

Today he is watching a room filled with extended family, friends, co-workers, neighbors and strangers; Rand had no clue who they were or how they knew Marie. He saw small groups of maybe three or four people huddled together talking, some

smiling, while others outright chuckled at something someone else in the group had said. These unknowns never came over to Rand and he didn't see them approach his and Marie's only child, Kenzie. He openly scowled at the nameless people. He knew one of them saw him make the face. She stared at him, her eyes widened, and then she glanced away to continue the conversation with the other unidentified people in her group. *Who the hell were they? And what did they find so funny? At a funeral? What level of disrespect was happening here?* Rand shifted in the Victorian-style chair and readjusted his long legs. He stuck one of his index fingers between his throat and necktie and pulled outward to give himself some more room to breathe. It seemed as if the room was getting warm and he was beginning to overheat. Rand was used to wearing a necktie every day, but for some reason, this tie felt as if he were being strangled and restricted.

The group of snickering people dispersed and seemed to be heading for the door leading to the parking lot. Rand saluted

them, wishing he had never observed them to begin with.

His eyes scanned the viewing room, bypassing Marie's

casket at the front of the room. His eyes were looking for

Kenzie; his nineteen-year-old daughter. The last time he

had seen her, she was talking to Josie Devlin, her best

friend since toddlerhood, and their next-door neighbor.

Josie had been a constant in all of their lives since her

family moved in almost two decades ago. He knew Kenzie

would be leaning on her friend more so now than ever.

Kenzie had just lost her mother, and Josie would be the

comfort that his daughter would be seeking. In Rand's

mind, Josie would be able to console his daughter more

than he ever could. He was still reeling from Marie's death.

Not seeing Kenzie floating from person to person playing

the perfect hostess, Rand pushed back in the chair and his

eyes settled on the white casket placed at the center of the

room. He'd been avoiding the wooden box for hours, but he

knew he couldn't avoid it much longer. After tonight, he'd

never see the casket, or Marie, again, and Rand wasn't sure how he'd get through tomorrow.

Rand placed his hands on his thighs and began tapping his fingers, a mindless movement to occupy his thoughts. As he continued the action with his fingers, he thought back to the night of Marie's death.

It was the evening of their twentieth wedding anniversary, and Rand had made reservations at their favorite Italian restaurant across town. He had told Marie earlier that morning that he'd be home in time to get ready for the evening, but as the day went on, Rand realized he'd have to stay at work finishing up grading the midterm papers from his students, so he texted Marie to tell her that he'd meet her at the restaurant at the reservation time. She was not happy and made her feelings known. A texting squabble ensued and Rand felt bad, but he needed to get these grades in by six o'clock that evening so they could be out into the system by his student aide, Lilly.

Marie had finally agreed to meet Rand at the restaurant separately, and the fighting stopped. Rand got lost in grading and when he saw that he only had ten minutes to get to the restaurant, he packed up his work, told Lilly to finish and he headed out the door of his office towards the parking lot.

Once his feet hit the pavement, he started jogging to his sedan on the other side of the staff parking lot. If he hurried, caught every green light and traffic was moving well, Rand figured he could be to the restaurant in under ten minutes and he wouldn't have to spend the first half hour of his and Marie's romantic dinner apologizing for his tardiness.

As he approached his car, Rand noticed a state police cruiser parked next to his vehicle. His attention was drawn away from the police car when his cell phone rang in his pocket. He retrieved it and looked at the screen; it showed Marie's face, his screen saver for her when she called him.

"Oh, just great," Rand muttered as he raised the phone to his ear. "I'm on my way now, just running a few minutes late."

"Mr. Randall Donovan?" came a man's vice.

"Yes, who is this?" Rand's steps faltered and he dropped his briefcase. He bent over to pick it up and asked, "Why are you calling from my wife's phone?"

"Mr. Donovan, this is State Trooper Christopher Godwin. I am parked outside by your vehicle.

I need to speak to you in person."

Rand looked back to the state police car in front of him and squinted his eyes. He was trying to see through the rear-tinted windows of the cruiser to see if he could see Marie in the backseat.

"Mr. Donovan? Are you still there?"

"Yes, I am. I'm coming up on your vehicle right now. Is my wife in the backseat? Has she been arrested?" Rand asked as his futile attempt to see through the darkened windows failed.

"Alright, we'll meet you at your car." The officer disconnected the call without answering Rand's questions.

Rand's feet stopped. He was about twenty yards from his sedan and he saw two state troopers exit their patrol car and head in his direction. Rand's first instinct was to run. *Wasn't that what people did with the police?* No, only guilty people did that and Rand had done nothing illegal. His eyes squinted as the two officers approached.

He slipped his phone back into his jacket's pocket and urged his feet to move, but he remained standing in the same spot. When the two officers closed the gap between them, Rand felt a sudden urge to sit down. His legs felt wobbly. His stomach was churning and his heart rate quickened.

"Mr. Donovan," the taller of the two officers spoke. "I'm Officer Godwin."

The other trooper remained silent, and only outreached his

hand that held a cell phone and offered it to Rand. Rand's hand moved on its own and took the device. Rand looked down at the phone; it was Marie's he knew for sure. It was encased in a bright pink cover. Rand would know that cover anywhere with its sparkling gems decorating one side.

"Wh-where's my wife?" Rand stuttered, still staring at the phone in his hand.

"There's been an accident, Mr. Donovan. We need to take you to the hospital."

"Is Marie, okay?" He glanced at Officer Godwin.

"Please, Mr. Donovan, we need to take you to the hospital where your wife's been transported."

Rand opened his mouth to reply, but he couldn't think of a word to say. Marie had been transported to a hospital, that was a good sign he thought.

"Let me get my car," Rand started and took a step towards his vehicle.

"I think it's best you come with us," Officer Godwin replied. "We can get you there faster."

Rand only nodded, slipped Marie's cell phone into his jacket's other pocket and followed the two officers back to their cruiser. The silent officer opened the rear passenger side door and Rand slid into it.

To this day, Rand barely recalled what all happened on the drive to the hospital across town. He remembered the scanner in the patrol car, he heard voices calling out police verbiage and a female speaking specific calls out to responding troopers, but Rand had no idea what any of the words meant.

It wasn't until the car pulled up to the emergency area of the hospital that Rand was snapped out of his reverie. When the officer opened his door, allowing Rand to exit the vehicle, his legs gave out and he stumbled. The officer grabbed ahold of his arm and helped him stand.

"Is my wife okay?" Rand spoke for the first time.

"The doctor will speak with you inside," Officer Godwin replied, and ushered Rand in the automated doors leading to the triage area. "Wait here."

Rand watched Officer Godwin walk up to the desk and speak with the nurse. He pointed in Rand's direction and he saw the nurse's face grow pale. Rand felt queasy. He swallowed hard and what happened next sent his world into a spiral downward.

Rand saw a doctor come through the swinging door and was directed by a nurse in Rand's direction. The doctor walked over, placed his hand on Rand's shoulder and began talking. Rand couldn't focus. He couldn't hear the doctor's words. Rand's focus was on the nurse who had escorted the doctor over. Her face was ashen and her blue eyes were shimmering with moisture. She looked into Rand's eyes and all Rand could see was her sadness and empathy.

"Do you understand, Mr. Donovan?" the doctor's voice broke into Rand's thoughts.

"What?" Rand was confused. "What... where's Marie? I want to see my wife..." Rand took a few steps in the direction of the exam rooms in the emergency care unit.

"Mr. Donovan, you cannot go back there yet," the doctor stepped in front of Rand to halt his progression. "Please, give us a few minutes to take care of your wife. A nurse will come out to get you when you can go back."

Rand wanted to hit the doctor. He wanted to knock the guy out and find his wife. Rand balled both his hands into fists and started to raise one of them when Officer Godwin grabbed his arm. Rand looked at the officer and lowered his arm.

"Mr. Donovan, that won't help the situation," Officer Godwin muttered. Rand raised his eyes and stared at the officer.

"I can't... I just can't..." Rand lost his balance and the two officers guided him to a chair.

As Rand slumped in the chair, his first thought was his final words to Marie were a promise to meet her at the restaurant. He didn't uphold and keep that promise. If he'd only stopped grading the papers and let Lilly do it. If he'd only gone home in time to pick Marie up as he promised. If he'd only given his wife as much attention as he did his job, maybe she'd still be alive. Maybe Kenzie would still have her mother.

Life was full of *what if's* and *if only's* and Rand had more than his fair share right now.

Rand shook off those thoughts and, not being able to find Kenzie or Josie in the crowd of mourners and well-wishers, Rand stood up and headed for the exit. He needed some fresh air and if he had to look at one more stranger or person smiling; he knew he'd lose it.

Rand opened the door, stepped out and inhaled deeply. The air filled his chest and he exhaled slowly. After doing this a few times, he began walking to the south area of the funeral home. He thought he had seen a sitting area near the back of the building.

Sticking his hands in his pants' front pockets, Rand strolled around the building. He saw a bench that was occupied by an older man. As much as Rand wanted to sit down, he didn't want to bother the man. Rand walked past the man, nodded at him and continued walking along the paved path.

"Sit with me," the older man called out when Rand was about ten feet past him.

"You sure," Rand inquired and glanced back at the man.

"Yes, yes. Sit, please," the man patted the spot beside him on the bench.

Rand turned around and walked back and hefted himself onto the bench with a loud sigh.

"Yes, yes," the man muttered. "I know what you mean. Today is the second worst day of my life. The first being the day my dear Frannie took her last breath last week."

"I'm sorry," Rand replied. "Not a good day at all."

"Your wife too?"

"Yes, she died on our twentieth anniversary," Rand answered.

"Life is too short," the man said and removed a silver flask from the inside of his suit jacket. He opened the top and raised it to his mouth. "This may help ease the pain of a broken heart, but it won't remove the memories," the man touched his temple with his free hand.

He took a long swallow and before putting the cap back on to seal the flask, he held it up to Rand; offering a swig. Rand, who rarely drank, even on a social level, didn't hesitate to take the proffered container. He raised it to his lips and took a long swallow. The alcohol burned going down his throat, but Rand didn't care. The discomfort of the liquor sliding down to his stomach gave him a momentary lapse in his thoughts of Marie.

"Have another," the man offered. "It'll not only numb your body, but it'll pierce through your memories, if only temporarily."

Rand raised the vessel to his mouth again and drank.

If could only feel this way continuously, then maybe he'd

forget about his guilt.

Chapter 1

Rand rolled over in his bed, causing a liquor bottle to drop

to the carpeted floor. He rubbed the sleep from his eyes as

his head pounded. Groaning, he stretched out in his king-size bed and tried to remember what day it was.

Tuesday? Friday? Rand attempted to ignore the throbbing and raised his hands to rub his temples. *Did he have class today?* Rand's eyes fluttered open and, moving his head slowly, he glanced at his alarm clock. The time read a few minutes after eight.

"Oh, crap," Rand sat up and shifted so his legs hung over his bed as he ground the palms of his hands into his closed eyes. His headache was worse than he could ever remember. He reached down, grabbed the liquor bottle and peeked at it. *Empty.*

"Damn it," he muttered.

Still unsure what day it was, Rand half considered flopping back into bed and sleeping more. Usually, his headaches went away if he slept more, but for some reason, he thought it could be Thursday. And if it were Thursday, then he had a class that started at 9 am.

Rand stood up, felt wobbly and steadied himself with one

hand on the nightstand and the other on the way adjacent to his bed. He waited a few seconds until he got his balance under control and went to his on-suite bathroom. He began rinsing his mouth out with mouthwash and as he spit the green liquid into the sink basin, his brain began functioning.

"Damn it! Today's Sunday." He dried his lips with a washcloth and headed back into his bedroom. He dropped into his bed and passed out before he could cuss about his headache again.

***

"Dad," Kenzie's voice infiltrated Rand's sleepy haze.

"Dad, are you awake?"

"Huh?" He rubbed his eyes, noticing his headache was minimal. "What?"

"It's almost noon," Kenzie replied. "You promised to take me and Josie to the Art Show at the Galleria today."

"Ugh," he muttered. Hi did recall making that promise a few weeks ago, but he had forgotten about it since that conversation.

"Dad," Kenzie's voice rose an octave. "You promised."

"I know, I know," he replied before she started whining in that late teen voice. "Give me twenty minutes to wake up, shower and get ready."

"Twenty minutes is all you have," Kenzie warned. "It opens at one and it'll take us at least thirty minutes to get there."

Rand had his eyes closed, but he could picture Kenzie hovering over him with her hands planted on her hips while she scowled at him.

"I'll make it fifteen then," he promised his daughter. "Now go, so I can get ready."

"I'm coming back up here in fourteen minutes," Kenzie forewarned him. He heard her walking towards the bedroom door. "I mean it, dad."

"I know," he replied and waited for her to leave the room and close the door.

Kenzie slammed the door in her wake and he opened his eyes. He waited a few seconds before sitting up, as he didn't want his headache to come back. That was the last thing he needed right now.

Kenzie held true to her word, just as Rand was heading out of his bathroom to go downstairs, Kenzie knocked on the door.

"You ready?"

Rand opened the door. "Just heading your way now. You and Josie ready to go?"

"Yup," Kenzie replied with a smile. "All ready."

Rand allowed Kenzie to go down the stairs first and as his

daughter headed into the living room, Rand took a turn into

his office. He shut the door, walked to his desk and opened

the bottom drawer. He removed his flask and grabbed a

half-empty fifth of vodka. He filled the flask with the clear

alcohol, making a mental note to stop and get more on the

way home without the girls knowing somehow, then he

twisted the lid on the portable container. He slipped it into

his jacket's inside breast pocket, put the almost empty

bottle back in his desk's drawer and headed out to meet the

girls.

***

Thankfully, Rand's head wasn't pounding too badly as he

drove across town to the art show. He had the radio tuned

to a news talk show and the girls sat in the backseat of his

sedan and talked and giggled through the streets. Their

melodious voices and laughter kept Rand company as he drove.

As their chatter continued, Rand took a few moments to reflect on his daughter and her best friend's relationship. Kenzie was an outgoing social butterfly; as Marie used to say, whereas Josie was a shy, homebody. He could recall many weekend nights when Kenzie had to practically drag Josie out to a party or gathering. Rand could see in Josie's face when those nights came around, how Josie's eyes pleaded with Kenzie to not make her go. Some days, Rand felt sorry for Josie always being lugged to some event or social gathering. Perhaps it was because he was a homebody himself. He found contentment when he was at home, or in his office grading student's papers. But Marie had been persistent and when she wanted to go out, she made it clear that she was going out.

Rand sighed at the memories of Marie. He had played different scenarios in his head ever since her death five months ago. Marie had wanted to go to their favorite Italian

restaurant that night, but earlier in the week, Rand had tried

to coerce Marie into just staying home and he would have

picked up their meals on his way home from the college.

But Marie had droned on and on about never being able to

go out on the town; as she referred to those rare occasions.

Eventually, growing tired of Marie's complaints, he gave in

and made the reservation.

Rand returned his attention between the road in front of

him and the girls behind him. Kenzie was laughing about

some party they had attended the night before and Josie

didn't look as animated. Her joyless frown told Rand she

didn't have as much fun as Kenzie did.

Rand's focus turned to how Kenzie resembled Marie with

her flowing blonde hair and blue eyes, and Josie, if his

memory recalled correctly, was a vision of her mother,

Alicia, with light chestnut hair and brown eyes. Rand had

never really paid much mind to Alicia; as he saw her as a

very blunt and to-the-point person, and for some reason that

irked Rand to no end.

He thought about when Josie's family had moved in next

door almost twenty years ago. Jon and Alicia walked over

to his and Marie's front yard two days after the Devlins had

moved in. Both Kenzie and Josie were within a few months

of each other and had instantly bonded over plastic teething

toys in Kenzie's playpen that had been moved outside to

the front lawn as Rand and Marie discussed how Marie

would reshape the front flowerbeds later in the summer.

Since that day, Kenzie and Josie were inseparable. Over the

years, Rand had witnessed how nothing, or anyone, would

ever come between the girls. If someone was bullying

Josie, Kenzie would step in and remind the tormentor that

they had to deal with Kenzie when Josie was hurt. Just as

Josie always came to Kenzie's rescue with academics,

grades, and studying. He recalls many late nights, that

turned into weekday sleepovers when a big test was coming

up and Josie would help Kenzie learn the periodic table or what years the Revolutionary War took place.

Kenzie and Josie leaned on each other and they would never allow anyone to come between them. Rand subconsciously put one hand over his breast and felt the hardness of his flask. He eased into a private solace knowing it was there.

For some unknown reason today, he had been thinking about Marie more often than in recent days. He wasn't sure as to why, but knowing he could lose himself and soften the emotional pain he was experiencing with his little bottle helped Rand ease up on his guilt.

***

Rand sat on a bench while Kenzie and Josie walked around

the art show. He'd never had an interest in art; especially this new-age art that he figured any toddler could create, so he decided to take it easy, find a spot to sit and let the girls have their day of fun.

Looking around the small exhibit room, Rand spotted a smaller bench in the corner and more discreet than the one he was sitting on now; which was in the center of the room and anyone could see him. He got up, strolled over to the little bench and slid onto the hard seat. He glanced around the room to see if anyone was watching him, and when he saw he was unnoticed, he slipped his flask out of his jacket and took a small swallow.

The alcohol slid down his throat and he instantly felt revived. The harsh burn he remembered from months ago didn't seem to bother him anymore. He took one more swig and then returned the vessel to his pocket. His eyes scanned the room, and he saw he was still concealed from anyone seeing him. He leaned back on the bench and waited for the girls to find him so they could head home. His flask was almost empty and he needed to stop at a liquor store and cautiously buy more alcohol.

Hours later, after returning home and from an impromptu pizza dinner with the girls, Rand goes to his office to settle in to grade some papers.

Earlier when they had been in the pizza parlor, he noticed the girls were eyeing some college boys at a nearby table, Rand used this opportunity to slip out, claiming he needed some antacids because the pizza wasn't agreeing with him, he went next door to a liquor store, bought two more fifths of Vodka and hid them under the driver's seat of his car. He returned to the pizza joint with no one the wiser.

Kenzie and Josie had taken up refuge in Kenzie's bedroom about an hour ago and Rand was looking over his student's papers in his home office. The new semester had just started two weeks ago, and Rand could already pick out certain students. He knew which ones were the "brown-nosers", he had the lazy ones pegged and he could even tell which ones were in his class but didn't want to be there.

But due to class sizes and other preferable English class choices, this last group of students ended up in his class unwillingly. He made a mental note of those kids and would keep an eye on them. They usually turned in sloppy work and hardly put any effort into their studies. He could almost imagine losing five percent of his class by next week.

Rand had just emptied a glass of vodka and set the tumbler in his desk drawer; where he always kept his drink hidden, but readily available when Kenzie knocked on his office door. She told him she was going to spend the night at Josie's house.

"I don't think that's a good idea, Kenzie," he replied. "It's a school night."

"Dad," she rolled her eyes. "Tomorrow is Monday and my first class isn't until eleven. I can sleep in and still be to class in time."

Instead of fighting this uphill battle, Rand agrees that she can go to Josie's for the night. He figured he'd get more work done with the girls out of the house than if he had been adamant about Kenzie going. If she stayed in the house, Kenzie would repeatedly bother him, he'd get frustrated and they would end up in another argument; Rand didn't think he could handle an argument tonight.

Ten minutes later, the girls were gone and Rand settled into his chair. He poured himself another drink and saluted the air, "Kenzie is right. My first class isn't until ten tomorrow morning, so let's enjoy the night."

He swallowed the entire tumbler of vodka and immediately refilled the glass. He grabbed his laptop and moved on to the next student's paper.

Chapter 2

Rand cursed under his breath after the last few straggling

students left his auditorium classroom. He was having a

bad day; one among a string of bad days seemed to have

settled into his life, and he was growing more impatient.

In his last class alone, he couldn't stay focused on the

material of the syllabus. He snapped in frustration at two

students and he finally lost all his composure when he saw

his flask was empty. He recalled filling it up that morning

before he left the house, but now it was dry.

"How the hell did that happen?" he muttered and kicked the

chair near his desk. The metal clanked on the floor and hit

the podium. The sound echoed through the room and Rand

ran his hands over his face.

Did he positively fill the flask all the way? Did some leak

out? Or did someone find it and take a few swigs?

He was doubting himself now and he didn't care much for

it. He slumped into his desk chair, tossed his head back and

shut his eyes, then retraced his morning routine in his mind.

After a few minutes, he knew he had refilled the flask to its

limit.

"So, did I take a few more sips than I remember?" he

whispered to the empty room. Thinking back to the last few

hours and classes, Rand never drank in front of his students

openly, but he did add a nip or two of alcohol to his coffee

mug in between classes to get him through the next set of

students.

He must've refilled his coffee mug an extra time or two. It had been a stressful morning, so he could imagine he had done that.

Rubbing the palms of his hands over his eyes, Rand didn't have another on-site class today, so he decided to pack up his laptop and papers and head home. He could finish up his work remotely. Grabbing what he needed, Rand scooped up his laptop satchel, briefcase and car keys and headed out to the parking lot. He shoved the keys in his pocket and exited the building.

He'd stop off at the corner liquor store, grab a bottle and head home. Maybe he'd stop off at that little sandwich shop that Kenzie raved about and he'd grab some dinner. That way neither of them would have to cook and Rand could focus on getting his mood straightened out.

As he approached the parking lot, he glanced over the college campus. He saw students walking, riding bikes and skateboards as well as many sitting on the lawns in front of different halls and buildings. His mind drifted to being young, carefree and having no responsibilities. He'd been that long ago and he missed those days.

Rand's eyes moved along the grassy area and he saw Josie. She was sitting alone on one of the dozens of park benches throughout the grounds. She had her oversized cello case leaning up against the bench and a backpack resting at her feet. She appeared to be dejected. Her face was pinched and she seemed to be staring off into space.

Rand reached into his car and set his laptop bag and briefcase on the roof of the sedan. He continued watching Josie as she raised a hand to her cheek and wiped away a tear.

"Damn it," Rand cursed.

He retrieved his car keys from inside his trouser's front pocket, all the while keeping his eyes on Josie. He should go over and see what she was visibly upset about and see if she needed anything. But he stood in place. If he did that then it would be that much longer before he could get to the store and then home.

"Oh cripes," he muttered. He started to return his car keys to his pocket when a young man approached Josie. Rand watched in anticipation. He knew the young kid. He had been in Rand's class last semester. But for some reason, Rand couldn't recall the kid's name.

Rand observed the young boy stop near Josie and start talking to her. Josie nodded her head and the boy sat down next to her. He slid his arm behind Josie, resting it along the bench's back. Josie smiled at the boy and the boy started talking. Rand saw Josie nod her head and reply. She talked non-stop and the boy sat and listened to her.

Rand felt a wave of relief. He wouldn't have to delay his trip to the liquor store, and it looked as if Josie had found someone to listen to her troubles. Rand applauded his hold-up in rushing over to Josie. She'd probably find better consoling from someone her age; or Kenzie later.

He unlocked his sedan, opened the door and gathered up the items he left on the roof and slid into the driver's seat. He started the car and began backing out of his assigned parking spot. He didn't bother with his seatbelt because the liquor store was just around the corner from the college.

***

"What the hell..." Rand cussed. He opened his eyes and he found himself sitting in the driver's seat of his car. The sun was cresting the horizon from in front of him, so he knew it was morning. *Did he stay out here all night? Did he even go into the house when he got home yesterday? Or did he just get home recently?*

He looked down and saw he was wearing the same pants and dress shirt that he wore to work yesterday. His cell phone was beeping a low battery signal in the passenger seat. Next to the phone was one empty bottle of whisky and an unopened fifth of vodka.

"Whisky," he slurred. "When did I start drinking whisky?"
Rand reached over to grab his phone and he moved a paper
bag that was laying beside the device. He heard glass
clanking inside and he looked in the bag. He saw four
empty sample bottles of brandy, whisky, vodka and gin
inside.

"No wonder you feel like crap, Donovan. You know better
than to mix drinks." his mouth was dry and tasted as if he'd
been eating some rancid garlic.

He looked up the driveway and saw the absence of
Kenzie's car. She must've stayed at a friend's house last
night. He glanced next door to Josie's place but didn't see
his daughter's car there either. With the little charge left in
his phone, he opened it up to see if there were any
messages from Kenzie. She had messaged him just before
midnight to say she was staying at a classmate's house and
she'd see him in the morning.

Rand looked at the time on his phone and saw it was just before eight o'clock. He had time to get inside, shower and clean up, then head off for his nine o'clock class. He needed to make it quick, as he didn't want Kenzie to pull into the driveway and see him like this.

He shoved the paper bag under his seat and took his car keys and phone and headed into the house. As he walked the pathway up to the front porch, he glimpsed at the neighborhood, making sure none of his neighbors were watching. He didn't see anyone walking about or peeking through their curtains as he entered his house.

Chapter 3

Kenzie has been getting so frustrated with Josie. Lately, her best friend seemed to be distracted more than usual. Every time Kenzie suggested they go out somewhere, to a party, a sporting event, or even just a gathering with classmates at a restaurant, Josie brushed off the invite and had some lame excuse.

There was a party at one of the fraternities that night, and Kenzie was anxious to go. She'd been looking forward to this party for weeks, and she wasn't going to let Josie ruin the night.

"Come on, Josie," Kenzie whined. "You haven't gone with me to the last two parties on campus."

Josie rolled her eyes and sighed. "Kenzie, I have tons of homework due on Monday and Tuesday. I need to get them done so I can get my grade up."

"Sheesh, Josie," Kenzie replied and threw up her hands. "Your grades, your grades. That's all I hear about now is your grades."

"Well, I'm not as fortunate as you," Josie said, looking up from her laptop. "I don't have free college. I had to get a scholarship and pay for the rest."

Kenzie felt her anger growing. Every time she questioned Josie about her studies and school, Josie tossed up the fact that Kenzie goes to college for free because her dad was a professor there. It was one of the perks Kenzie received.

"Josie, stop it," Kenzie sighed. "All I want to do is go to this party with you. We haven't been out together in weeks and I miss having you around." Kenzie flung herself down on Josie's bed and stared at the ceiling.

Josie stood up and flopped down next to Kenzie. They lay there in silence for a few moments. Kenzie knew Josie was smart and could easily get straight A's in any class she took, so she didn't understand why this American Literature class was so difficult for her friend and why she was struggling.

"I understand you take your grades seriously," Kenzie said. "And I also know that you feel you need to focus on your schooling, but it's just one night. One evening going to a party."

"Kenzie, how about this?" Josie began. "Let me work this weekend and I promise, *completely promise*, that the next party I will go to with you."

Kenzie sighed, propped herself up on her elbows, and looked at her friend. "This is the last time," Kenzie warned. "The next party you bail on me for, you can consider our friendship over."

Josie glanced over at her and smiled. "Yeah, yeah, how many times have I heard that before?"

"As many times as you've ditched me for homework," Kenzie laughed.

***

Kenzie tied her hair up in a messy bun with a few long tendrils of hair floating down and resting on her shoulders and neck. She took one final glance in the mirror, satisfied with how she looked, she grabbed her clutch purse and headed out of her room. She bounced down the stairs and stopped at her dad's home office door. Within a second, he called out to her after she knocked.

"Hey, dad," she replied as she flung the door open. "I'm heading out."

"Mmm," he muttered, with his focus now really on her, but on his laptop. "Where are you going?"

"To the party at the Chi Psi," she answered.

"Is Josie going with you?"

Kenzie sighed and shifted on her feet. "No, not tonight."

"Again? She's not going," her dad glanced up from his laptop. "Is she sick?"

"No," she replied. "Homework, her grades, *blah-blah-blah*... same old excuse."

"Give her a break, Kenzie," her dad defended Josie. "She's working hard, I'm assuming."

"Dad," Kenzie moaned. "You sound just like her."

"Why?" her dad asked. "Because she takes her education

seriously?"

Kenzie rolled her eyes. "And I don't?" She challenged her

dad.

"I never said that. You did," he responded, ignoring her

attitude.

"I won't be home too late," she told her dad, wanting to

change the subject quickly and get out of the house before

this conversation turned into either a full-blown discussion

of her future or worse, an argument.

She noticed her dad had already returned his attention to his

laptop, so she took this as a sign to slip out before he

noticed she had gone.

As she shut his office door, her dad yelled out, "Don't be

late!"

"I won't," Kenzie shook her head. She swore every day

since her mother's death that her dad had gone deeper and

deeper into his world. He wasn't the same person now as he

had been six months ago.

***

Kenzie sat on the cement front porch steps that lead into the Chi Psi fraternity house and felt another wave of nausea erupting in her stomach. She placed both her hands on her abdomen and wished it to go away.

"Please, go away," she whispered. She hadn't had this much alcohol in quite some time and it was affecting her in a bad way. "Ugh," her mouth had begun watering, and she knew this was not a good sign.

"Here, try sucking on this," one of the fraternity guys handed her a candy.

Kenzie opened the roll of what smelled like peppermint and placed one of the hard candies in her mouth.

"Thanks," she muttered and handed him back the remaining roll of candy.

"They say peppermint helps calm the stomach and ease

nausea," he said and sat down next to her. He held out his

hand. "Grayson McDermott."

She continued sucking on the candy, looked at his

outstretched hand, and shook his hand. "Kenzie Donovan."

"Nice to meet you, Kenzie Donovan," he looked into her

eyes. "Any relation to Professor Donovan?"

"Yes, he's my father. But don't hold that against me," she

replied and noticed the queasy feeling in her stomach had

started to dissipate. She pointed to her mouth. "Seems as

though the candy is helping."

"Not a cure-all by any means, but it gets you through some

of the rough stuff, you know," he smiled and placed his

hands on his knees. "By yourself?"

Kenzie opened her mouth to reply *yes* but thought better of

it. She didn't know this guy.

"No, my friend is here too," she answered. "She's inside. I

just came out here to get some fresh air and hope to settle

my stomach."

"Gotcha," he said and looked behind him at the front door leading into the house. "Wanna go back inside now that you're feeling better and get something to eat?"

"Eww," she grimaced. "I'll go back inside, but nothing to eat for me."

"Yeah, I get it," he smiled and stood up, offered her his hand and she took it so he could help her stand. "But I bet you'll change your mind once you see the delicacies we have."

"Doubtful," she smiled back. "But one never knows."

They went back into the house and Kenzie glanced at her phone. It wasn't even eleven o'clock. She'd been having fun at the party and socializing with almost everyone who was there, but she still missed having Josie with her.

She followed Grayson into the dining area that was open to a massive kitchen. People stood all around the kitchen, leaning against the counters, laughing and drinking from plastic cups. She saw a few people she had already met and

talked with throughout the evening. A few smiled at her

and others gave a little wave.

She nodded in acknowledgment and turned back to

Grayson, who was filling a plastic plate with hors

d'oeuvres and other finger foods. He popped a meatball in

his mouth and chewed as he picked u a napkin.

"Sure, you don't want any," he offered.

"Positive," Kenzie said and held up her hand. "None for

me."

Grayson held up his and used it to direct Kenzie into the

living room. They walked over to a sofa that was

unoccupied and sat down. Grayson picked up some kind of

tortilla roll and ate it. He wiped his mouth with the napkin

and leaned closer to her.

"How's the candy doing?"

"I'm surprised, but it seems to be working," she smiled.

"Good," he said and continued eating off his plate.

Kenzie and Grayson sat on the sofa for hours, talking. Over time, Kenzie had indulged in a few more cups of beer and was having an issue seeing straight. She excused herself from Grayson and went to the bathroom. She dug out her cell phone from her purse and dialed her dad's number.

It rang and rang and when it went to his voicemail, Kenzie cussed at him. She pulled up Josie's number and called her. She answered on the second ring.

"Hey, how was the party?"

"I'm still here but I need you," Kenzie slurred.

"Oh man, Kenzie. How much have you had to drink?" Josie asked.

"I-I don't know," Kenzie felt overwhelmed and emotional.

"Can you... can you come..."

"I'll be there in ten minutes," Josie cut her off. "Where are you now?"

"In the b-bathroom," Kenzie replied and rubbed her forehead. She sat down on the toilet seat as the room started to spin. "Hurry, I don't feel so good."

"I'm heading out the door now," Josie said. "Stay on the phone with me until I get there."

"Mm-okay," Kenzie muttered.

The two girls talked as Josie drove across town to pick her up. Kenzie had no idea what they talked about, and when Josie arrived outside, she told Kenzie to stay in the bathroom and that she'd come inside and find her.

Seconds later, there was a knock on the bathroom door. Kenzie didn't feel as though she could stand and walk to open it.

"Kenzie, you in there," Josie's voice reverberated through the door.

"Y-yes," she muttered.

"Okay, I'm coming in," Josie replied and opened the door. "You, okay?"

"Not really," Kenzie breathed heavily. She looked at her friend and saw Grayson standing behind Josie. Kenzie tried to smile, but her stomach was recoiling. "I feel awful."

"It's okay," Josie replied and stepped into the bathroom.

She walked over to Kenzie and placed her arm around her

and helped her stand. "Let's get you home."

Kenzie leaned on Josie, who guided her out of the

bathroom and through the house. Grayson opened the front

door and helped Josie get Kenzie to the car. He opened the

car's passenger door and Josie got Kenzie seated and

fastened the seatbelt.

"Thank you," Josie said to Grayson.

"Anytime," he looked at Kenzie. "Find me at school next

week or here. Let me know you're okay."

"Yeah, sure," Kenzie waved her hand at him. "Onward,

Josie. Home, please."

Josie circled the front of the car and got in. She started the

engine and drove towards their cul-de-sac. Kenzie kept her

hands on her stomach and cursed herself for drinking more

alcohol, especially since the peppermint candy Grayson had

offered her had worked to tame her nausea.

"Got any peppermint candy?" she asked Josie.

"What? No. Why?"

"It helps calm down my belly," Kenzie sighed and laid her head back on the seat. "Grayson, that's the guy who escorted us out. Grayson McDermott. He gave me a peppermint candy earlier and it stopped me from puking."

"That was nice of him," Josie chided. "But why are you sick again?"

"Oh, you know," Kenzie lulled her head from side to side. "I was feeling better and having fun, so I had a few more drinks."

Josie clucked her tongue. "And now look at you. Sick again. Bad choice," Josie added, sounding like an old Mother Hen.

"Don't start, Jo," Kenzie hissed. "I don't need mothering."

Josie remained quiet as they pulled into the Devlin driveway. "Can you make it into your house? Or do you need help?"

"I'm f-fine," Kenzie slurred. "You just get on home now

and do that homework. I expect nothing less than an A

from you, young lady."

"Kenzie..." Josie whispered.

"I mean it," Kenzie reaffirmed. "Go home. I can make it."

Josie turned off the engine and put her keys in her pocket as

Kenzie opened the passenger door and stumbled out.

"Kenzie..."

"Go inside, Josie. I'm fine," she replied and headed across

the lawn leading to her front porch. After she climbed the

stairs, Kenzie looked back at Josie and waved her on. Josie

waved back and headed into her own house.

It took a few attempts to get her key into the lock so she

could open the front door, but eventually, Kenzie did it.

She entered the house and held her finger to her lips and

shushed herself to be quiet. The last thing she wanted was

to wake up her dad.

She had just placed her foot on the first step leading

upstairs when she heard her dad's voice call out from his

office.

Kenzie cursed under her breath and looked into the opened

door.

"I asked you, are you drunk?" her dad's voice was loud and

vibrated in her head.

"I had a few drinks," Kenzie chose not to lie.

Her dad got up from behind his desk and wobbled to where

Kenzie was standing. "What the hell, Kenzie! You could've

gotten into an accident. Why didn't you call me?"

"Call you?" Kenzie could smell alcohol in the air. While

she wasn't sure if it was coming from her, or her dad, she

didn't care. The way he said she should have called him

pissed her off. "I did try to call you."

"What? No, you didn't. I hope you didn't drive home in

this state," his words sounded slurred. *Or was it her*

hearing?

"Look at your phone," she yelled. "I called. You didn't

answer."

She watched her dad dig his phone out of his pocket and

check for her missed call.

"Sorry, I must've been sound asleep when you tried," he

apologized.

Kenzie took a few steps closer to him and could smell the

alcohol on his breath. She had only had beer at the party

and the stench she smelled was liquor. Whisky maybe.

"Have you been drinking?" she accused her dad.

"I'm an adult," he roared. "You are not. You're not of legal

drinking age."

"Oh, yeah," Kenzie giggled. "I forgot."

"Kenzie, this behavior is not like you..."

"Stop it, dad!" she yelled. "Just stop with the

sanctimonious parenting."

"Excuse me?"

"You heard me," Kenzie screamed. "You're about to give

me some high and mighty talk about drinking when you

yourself are drunk. You couldn't even answer your damn

phone to come get me."

"I'm an adult, Kenzie, and I was drinking at home, not

driving," he told her.

"Oh, so that makes it better, huh?" She challenged him.

"What if I was in trouble, dad? What if I had been

assaulted? Or worse..."

"Kenzie, we're not having this discussion right now,

we're..."

"Both too drunk?" She finished his sentence.

"Kenzie!"

"Oh, stop it, dad," she seethed. "You need to get your head

out of your ass. I've seen you drinking when you think I'm

not looking."

Her dad's face seemed to glow a hot red. She knew she had

hit a "button" that was a trigger to him.

"You need to stop drinking your sorrows away," she added.

"What the hell would mom think about your behavior if she were still alive?"

In a split second, her dad raised his hand and slapped her across the face. Kenzie raised her hand and placed it on her cheek where her dad had just struck her.

"What the hell!" She screamed. She stared at her father, then turned and ran up the stairs. As she ran to her room, she heard her father call her name. She slammed the door and fell onto her bed, crying.

Chapter 4

Weeks later...

Over a long weekend break, Rand is hard at work on his tenure review application when there's a knock at the front door. Groaning at the interruption, he goes to see who's here. He took a long swallow of the Vodka in his half-empty glass before setting it in his desk drawer. Glancing at his desk as he walked away, he made sure the fifth of vodka wasn't left out.

He knows that Kenzie wouldn't hear the knock from upstairs, nor would she come down and risk facing him. But she wasn't home. She had gone somewhere hours ago; never telling him where or when she'd be back.

Since that fateful night when Kenzie had come home from the Chi Psi party and Rand had slapped her across the face for being a rebellious immature child, to be honest, he had been avoiding her just as much.

As he walked to the front door, Rand thought about the last few weeks. Kenzie was never home, and when she was, he never caught sight of her. She was an elusive "roommate" to him. When he was on the main level of the house, Kenzie was upstairs. When he went upstairs, she snuck down to the main level. She couldn't even bear to be anywhere near him.

Not that Rand didn't blame her. He'd probably behave the

same way if someone had slapped him. His behavior had been abhorrent.

The following morning, he had woken up feeling ashamed and guilt-ridden for his action. He had wanted to talk to Kenzie and explain how her words had sent him over the edge and to apologize for his behavior, but when he went to her bedroom door to have the conversation, she had ignored his knocks and, after a few minutes, told him to go away and she had nothing to say to him. He knew the event was still fresh for Kenzie, but he did want her to know how sorry he was, but her refusal to talk told him she wasn't ready to hear his excuses or apology.

Rand opened the front door to see Josie standing there with a backpack. She looked lost. He noticed her.

"Hey, Josie," he spoke. "Sorry, but Kenzie isn't home."

"That's okay," she smiled. "I'm actually here to see you. I need some advice."

"Oh," he was shocked. "Come on in."

Josie entered the foyer and went into the living room. She set her backpack on the end table as Rand shut the front door. He followed her into the room and offered her a seat on the sofa. He joined her on the opposite end of the sofa and rested his forearms on his knees, and clasped his hands together.

"So, what advice are you needing?" He asked and looked over at her. He glimpsed over her shoulder to his office doorway and thought he should've finished the last swig of his vodka. He kept his fingers entwined as a way to keep the shaking under control.

Josie unzipped her backpack and pulled out a folder. She sifted through some of the papers and put the folder on the coffee table while keeping a couple of papers in her hand. "I have a problem with my scholarship," she started, her voice cracking as if she would cry at any second. "And I don't know what to do about it."

"Okay," Rand replied. "Isn't this something you should be

discussing with your counselor?"

"I have," she answered. "Three times, but he isn't being very helpful."

"So, how can I help?"

Josie glanced at the papers in her hand and explained how she had to keep a certain GPA to maintain her scholarship and how one course, an American Literature course, was causing her GPA to dip below the required number.

"If I don't get that grade up another percentage point, I'll lose my scholarship," Josie explained. "If I lose it, I'll have to drop out."

Rand had listened to Josie talk for the last half hour. He was impressed with her knowledge of how the scholarship worked and how much research she had done. He let her finish talking and took in the fact that she may have to drop out of college and how devastating that would be to her and her parents.

"I just don't know what else to do," a tear fell on her cheek;

which she immediately wiped away.

"And you've spoken with Dr. Allen about this?"

Josie nodded. "She just said I need to apply myself harder to bring up the grade in her class. But I swear, Mr. Donovan, I've done everything I can think of to do that."

Rand believed her when she said she'd been trying to bring her grade up. He knew, from stories from Kenzie, just how much homework, extra credit, and studying Josie did every week. He also knew Jackie Allen, the American Literature professor, could be a harsh grader. She didn't believe in the Bell Curve on hard subjects and she could have favorites, and not-so-favorites, every semester. In Rand's opinion, somehow Josie had fallen into the non-favorite category.

"I have less than two months to bring that grade up, or it's *bye-bye* scholarship," Josie sobbed. "I've been rehearsing how I'll tell my parents, and none of the conversations in my head go well."

Rand sat back and knew the semester had just begun and he

formulated an idea. He looked at Josie, who had such innocence and hopefulness in her blue eyes. In all the years he'd known Josie, he had never noticed just how beautiful her blue eyes were. They were what his grandmother would have called cornflower blue, with a hint of green if you looked close enough; and Rand was sitting close enough to see the green flecks.

"Josie, what if I were to request a transfer for you?" Rand asked. "I can do a student transfer request and have you put into my class. I know the topic may not be in your normal realm of American Literature, but I can promise you, I am not a hard professor, demand perfection, but I do grade on the Bell Curve which many students appreciate."

Josie's eyes appeared to light up, enhancing the green to a brilliant emerald color. "Oh, Mr. Donovan, that would be wonderful!" She leaned over and hugged him. "I would be *so grateful* if you would and could do that."

Rand held Josie for a brief moment and something stirred

from deep within him. When she pulled away, he saw her smile of gratitude and he returned the grin.

"It's not a done deal yet," Rand replied when they separated. "I'll get the paperwork filled out and turned in tomorrow online and maybe I'll get an answer Monday when classes resume."

"Oh, Mr. Donovan, you are a Godsent!" She laughed, wiped away what he assumed were tears of happiness now and clapped her hands. "I knew coming to you was what I needed to do."

Rand felt a bliss release within him from Josie's compliments and enthusiasm. He couldn't remember the last time someone had given him such appreciation and accolades. His confidence seemed to need that boost. Dealing with Kenzie and the drama of that night, and he was still reeling from Marie's death, Rand hadn't noticed how much he'd been missing a simple gesture of recognition until Josie's words.

It was getting later in the afternoon and neither Rand nor Josie had eaten lunch, so they decided to have some food delivered. They spent the next hour talking about life in general and Josie shared her aspirations to continue her music degree and one day be an elementary school music teacher. Rand could envision Josie working with young schoolchildren. She had such a natural, lively personality and he could see children being drawn to her.

They had finished eating the Thai food from their delivery and were just sitting in the living room when Kenzie appeared in the doorway. She had entered the house without their knowledge. Josie's laughter from a lame *dad joke* that Rand had just told muffled Kenzie coming through the front door.

Kenzie made eye contact with Rand, and he could feel the cold stare. Her eyes felt as if they were burrowing into his soul. She never spoke a word. Her eyes went from Rand to Josie, and Kenzie's leer didn't soften when she looked at her friend.

Rand started to open his mouth to say something to his daughter, but she spun on her heels and stormed up the stairs. Seconds later, her bedroom door slamming shut echoed through the house.

"Oh my," Josie whispered. She set her napkin down on the coffee table that she had been using to dry the tears from her eyes when she had been laughing moments earlier. "I-I should..." Josie stood up and headed up the stairs to see Kenzie.

Rand sighed and stood up to begin cleaning up the lunch mess that he and Josie had made. He carried the empty containers to the kitchen and then headed back for the other garbage. As he walked back into the living room, he caught a glimpse of Josie leaving out the front door.

He went back into the kitchen to toss out the garbage when Kenzie spoke from behind him.

"Are you seriously behaving like this?"

Surprised by hearing his daughter's voice, Rand stopped

and turned to look at his daughter. He wasn't sure what she

was referring to.

"Excuse me," he said.

"You... and Josie, dad," Kenzie's voice oozed sarcasm.

"What? Me and Josie," he asked.

Kenzie rolled her eyes; a movement Rand was growing to

despise.

"You and Josie? Having lunch?"

"And..." he prodded her to explain.

"Seriously, dad," she sighed so loud Rand swore the

windows rattled.

"No, Kenzie. Not seriously. What are you saying?"

"You and Josie, alone here and the look of surprise on her

face when I showed up?" Kenzie was really pushing Rand

with this inquisition.

"Are you accusing me of doing something with Josie?" He

asked in disbelief and took a few steps closer to his

daughter. This was the last topic he figured would be their first conversation in weeks.

"Well, duh, dad," her attitude was grating on his nerves.

"Kenzie, that is way out of line," he growled at his daughter. "I can't believe that thought would ever cross your mind."

"Well, it crossed my mind because I come home and here you are, with my best friend, alone in the house, and it sure looked like you were both having a good ol' time," Kenzie spat.

"Jesus, Kenzie," Rand bellowed. "You can't be serious. I've been alone with her before. What has gone off kilter in your head that makes you think I'd be... that me and Josie..."

"Stop it, dad," she roared. "It was pretty obvious that I interrupted something..."

"Kenzie," Rand rumbled. "Nothing was obvious. Josie came over and needed some advice. Time got away from us and we were hungry. End of story."

Kenzie crossed her arms and glared at him. He could see

the anger, and a little disbelief, in her eyes. She stepped

away from him and walked to the doorway leading to the

living room and stopped.

"You better hope not, dad, 'cause I'll make sure to tell her

dad that you're wanting to get with his daughter," she

hissed and stormed out of the room. Seconds later, he heard

the front door slam shut.

Rand felt his anger advancing. He stalked to his office and

ripped open his desk drawer where his stash was located.

He grabbed the fifth of vodka he had opened earlier that

morning and sloshed it into his tumbler. He raised it to his

mouth and swallowed the entire glass of liquor.

He slumped into his chair and poured himself another

healthy glassful of alcohol and thought about the scene

between him and his daughter, and how her accusation felt

like a knife to his heart. How could she even think such a

thing would be happening? He was still mourning Marie's death, *wasn't he*?

He mulled over that question for a few minutes. When he had been talking with Josie and eating their meal, he never once thought of Marie. He never once, except for the initial shaky hands when they first sat down hours ago, wanted to drink. Liquor hadn't crossed his mind one time.

Rand considered that fact. They sat with each other. He glanced at his wall clock, for a good four hours and he never reached for a drink. He raised his glass to his mouth and took a sip. Josie had a way about her that made Rand forget about time and his work frustrations. But it was the way Marie never entered his mind during Josie's entire visit.

Rand didn't know what that meant, but it made him curious if it would happen again.

Chapter 5

Josie was packing up her laptop, school folders, and a light lunch. She only had two classes today, but they were four hours each. Today was the first day she'd be attending Mr. Donovan's 19th Century Poetry class and she was anxious to get the day started. She still couldn't believe he was able to get her transferred to his class. He was a lifesaver in Josie's eyes. She knew she would have lost her scholarship if he hadn't intervened.

Josie put her brown paper bag lunch into her backpack just as her dad came into the kitchen.

"Heading out to class?" he asked as he poured a cup of coffee.

"Yes," she smiled.

"You seem in a good mood," her dad replied. "I'll admit for a little while over the last week or so, I've been concerned with you."

"What?" Josie asked. She had no clue of her dad had picked up on her sullen behavior. As much as she had tried to hide her sour disposition and the uncertainty of her scholarship, it was evident her best effort had failed. "You noticed?"

Her dad chuckled and took a sip of his coffee. "Hard not to when you're stomping around, sighing all the time and not very enthusiastic on a Monday morning. I think today's the first day I've seen you smile since the new semester began."

"Well," Josie hadn't told her parents about the issue with her scholarship. She thought she'd wait until she had it all worked out before telling them the story.

There were many reasons for her hiding the fact that she could lose it. One being, she didn't want to look as if she wasn't smart enough to maintain her GPA. Second, she didn't want to inflict worry, or even the chance of financial hardship upon her parents to have to pay for her schooling. Finally, she wanted to show her parents she was mature and could handle tough situations on her own.

"Is something wrong?" her dad inquired, setting his coffee cup on the kitchen counter.

"No,' Josie replied and smiled. "I mean, there was a problem, but I took care of it."

"What problem?"

"It's nothing now," she replied. "It was something last week, but I handled it."

"Care to share, after the fact," her dad prodded a real answer.

"I have a few minutes." Josie glanced at the wall clock

behind her dad. "I was struggling in a class..."

"What?" her dad was surprised. "That's not like you."

"I know, dad. Trust me, I know," she sighed. "But I took the problem, figured it out and with the help of Mr. Donovan late last week, he was able to help me get it all sorted out."

"Mr. Donovan?" Her dad wrinkled his forehead at the mention of Kenzie's dad. "Why didn't you come to me... or your mother?"

"Honestly," Josie began. "I was kind of embarrassed to tell you."

"How bad could the problem have been for you to feel that way, honey?"

Josie sighed and looked away from her dad. She focused her line of vision out the kitchen window facing their backyard. She knew she had offended and hurt her dad by not going to him with her dilemma; she could see it in his face.

"It was bad enough," she replied. "I was having trouble with one class and the professor. It was going to affect my scholarship, and I was scared."

"Your scholarship," her dad's voice was filled with concern now. "What do you mean?"

"I was struggling with the GPA and I knew if I didn't bring up the grade quickly, I'd be in a situation of losing my scholarship."

Her dad considered her words and remained silent for a moment.

"So, how did Mr. Donovan come to our rescue?"

"He filled out transfer paperwork and got me out of the class and moved to his class, starting today."

"And how does that help to save your scholarship?"

"Honestly, I'm not sure yet, but I have hopes that 19th Century Poetry will be easier for me to comprehend than American Literature. The professor wasn't giving me any slack and was making the course difficult for others; not just me."

"So, you're hoping Mr. Donovan will give you this *slack* you need and you'll have a better GPA?" her dad's accusation of laziness was coming through.

"No, dad," she asserted. "I didn't go to him with that in mind, being transferred to his class. I went to him to ask how to handle possibly losing my scholarship and how I could reapply for a new one."

"And he changed the topic from that to getting you transferred to his class?"

"Well, yeah, I guess so," Josie replied.

Her dad's next words lingered in the silence. Josie looked at his face again and he seemed in deep thought. Not sure what to say next, she waited.

"Is there anymore to the story?" her dad inquired in a serious tone.

"Meaning what?" Josie had a feeling where her dad was going with the question, and as much as she didn't want to believe it, she waited for him to elaborate.

"Is that the only reason Mr. Donovan transferred you to his class? Has he ever indicated something... more than you just being a student?"

There it was! Josie was in disbelief. *Had her dad just accused her best friend's dad, their neighbor and a man who she had known her entire life of being promiscuous with her?*

"Wow, dad!" Josie wailed. "Seriously? How can you even think that? Mr. Donovan is like a second dad to me!"

"Josie, I'm just trying to figure out why he did what he did."

"Maybe it's because he knows how important my education is," she retorted. "Maybe it's because he was trying to help me out of a situation that I couldn't figure out on my own."

"Josie, there's no reason to be so brash," her dad scolded her behavior. "I was just asking a simple question that needed to be asked."

"Geez, dad," Josie rolled her eyes. "I go to someone who happens to be my best friend's dad, in need of help, where he just so happens to be a professor and has the knowledge to help and you get all *what's he after* on me!"

"Josie," her dad warned her of her brazen attitude. "How do you think it looks? He gets you transferred to his class. You never come to me, your father, for help, and all of a sudden you look like you're floating on cloud nine."

"I don't have time for this conversation," Josie replied and flung the backpack on her shoulder. "We'll talk when I get home, if you're here and have time for me."

Josie spun on her heels and marched to the back door. She opened it, walked through the threshold, and slammed it in her wake. She trudged down the driveway to her compact car. Once inside the vehicle, she started the engine and fumed about what had transpired between her and her dad, and how he had accused Mr. Donovan of possibly taking advantage of her.

Josie glanced at the Donovan's house. She saw Kenzie's

car in the driveway, but Mr. Donovan's sedan was gone.

It was true when she had gone over there last week to talk

to Mr. Donovan that she was inquiring if it would be

possible to re-apply for a new scholarship; or what the

other possibilities could be if she were to lose this one. So,

when he offered to transfer her and help her, Josie took his

offering as an easy solution that would save her. She never

once considered he had presented the transfer as a way to

get in her good graces, or for any other reason.

"Where the hell did dad get that idea?" she said to herself.

"How twisted is his mind?"

She backed out of the driveway and headed towards school.

As she drove, she contemplated her dad's accusation. The

more she thought about his words regarding Mr. Donovan,

the more she appreciated her friend's dad for helping. He

was just helping her, *right?* He was being paternal, *right?*

Josie knew he would have done the same for *any* other

student that he was helping. She could guarantee that.

She'd heard how he had helped his students keep their GPAs up, and how he assigned special assignments catering to a student with learning disabilities. He was a kind-hearted person. He was no promiscuous professor that lurked in the dark shadows, ready to pounce on an unsuspecting female student.

Josie shook her head as she pulled into the student parking lot. She turned the ignition off and sighed.

She remembered a few days ago when he had called her and said the transfer was a success and that she could attend his class today. She was so happy. She thanked him profusely and throughout the last few days; she had been thinking about how grateful she was to Mr. Donovan. He had helped her and she would have to repay him.

She spent Sunday afternoon thinking of how to show her gratitude, and all she could come up with was to make him something. Maybe a batch of cookies. Perhaps a small cake. One thing she knew for sure, she couldn't take him out anywhere or have dinner alone with him.

Last week, when they had sorted out her scholarship dilemma and were enjoying dinner and chatting, Kenzie showed up and ruined the entire day of celebration.

When Kenzie appeared in the doorway and looked pissed off, all Josie could do was follow her friend upstairs and talk about what she had walked in on. Josie was surprised when Kenzie flung out almost the same allegation that Josie's dad had just done. Josie found the quarrel with her best friend almost too much to handle and a real downer after the great day she had shared with Rand...

"Rand? Where did that come from?" Josie muttered. "It's Mr. Donovan, not Rand."

Josie shook her head and headed off to class. She needed to stop muddling her mind with all these condemnations from Kenzie, and now her dad.

She hefted the backpack on her shoulder and headed off to

19th Century Poetry. She wasn't going to allow the fight

with her dad to ruin her first day.

Chapter 6

Rand raked up the last of the leaves that were in the garden beds and his mind drifted to Marie. She loved to garden and was always out here weeding, digging, and making the curb appeal of their home spectacular. She'd spend all day on Sunday out here. Since her passing, Rand had neglected the yard work, but he decided today that he needed to at least rake out all the dead leaves.

He stopped raking, placed his hand on the rake's handle and wiped his brow with a rag he had found in the garage. It was a balmy afternoon with overcast skies, but he was breaking a sweat.

He wished he had brought out his flask. He could use a drink right now. Rand saw his neighbor, Jon Devlin, coming across his own lawn and headed toward him.

"Hey, neighbor," Rand greeted Josie's dad.

"Hi, Rand," he nodded in the direction of the cleaned-out flower beds. "Getting a head start on the season?"

"Sort of," he answered, and looked at his handiwork.

"Figured today was as good of a day as any."

"Yeah, Alicia's been after me to get her garden out back tilled up and ready for planting." Jon crossed his arms over his broad chest.

Rand nodded his head. He could recall every first of April how Marie would be insistent on him getting outside and helping her with the gardening chores and setup of the flower beds as well as the other areas around the yard.

"How's Kenzie doing?" Jon inquired.

"Good, I suppose," Rand didn't elaborate. No sense in gossiping and letting the neighbors know he and his daughter weren't exactly on speaking terms.

"Yeah," he muttered. "If she's anything like Josie, she's a spitfire and makes life a little less fun."

"Ain't that the truth," Rand agreed. He wiped his brow again. He didn't know why he was sweating and his mouth had grown dry. He cursed himself again for not bringing his flask out here with him.

"Hey," Jon began. "I heard Josie came to you a couple of weeks ago with a problem and..."

Rand wondered why Jon stopped mid-sentence. He glanced at his neighbor and waited for him to finish his thought, but when he didn't, Rand picked up the queue and replied.

"Yeah, she was having some issues with another professor and was hoping I could help her figure out the best solution." Rand felt no need to tell Jon about Josie's scholarship. He didn't know if she had told her parents, and Rand didn't want to be a snitch.

"Mmm..." was Jon's response.

"I hope that was okay." Rand didn't know how else to reply to Jon's grumble.

"Oh, yeah, yeah," Jon finally answered. "I just didn't know she was having a school problem."

"Well, you know how the girls can be," Rand chuckled and tried to make light of the issue.

"Yeah, they are fickle things," Jon replied, but amusement was not in his voice.

"Was there something else?" Rand asked, already knowing the answer. There was something off with Jon's body language. He seemed suspicious or skeptical.

"Well, now that you mention it," Jon started and shifted on his feet. "When I had started to talk to her the other morning, she was different."

"Different?" Rand inquired. "Different how?"

"Over the last few weeks, I noticed Josie was down and not happy," Jon began. "But the other morning, she was happy and seemed to be out of her funk."

"Okay," Rand listened.

"Anyway, when I asked her about her change in mood, your name came up," Jon's voice seemed a little on edge to Rand.

"My name?" Rand was confused. "Well, did say that she told you she had come to me to ask for some guidance?"

"That's all you offered, right?" Jon probed.

"What?" Rand was surprised by Jon's implication. "What the hell are you implying?"

"Rand," Jon began and held his hands up. "I'm just asking."

"I don't know what Josie told you, but we talked about her class and I offered to help her get transferred into mine," Rand growled.

"And why would you do that?" Jon asked. "Because you *wanted to help?*"

"Watch your step," Rand warned him and took a few steps closer.

"Or what?" Jon held his chin up.

"Jon, I'm warning you," Rand hissed.

"Were you only trying to help my daughter? Or did you have an ulterior motive?" Jon pushed the accusation.

"Your daughter came to me, Jon," Rand reminded him. "I didn't go to her."

"So, now you're saying my daughter is..."

"Jon!" Alicia screamed from behind her husband. "Stop it!"

Jon looked back at his wife, who was now walking across their driveway and standing on the edge of the property line.

"Stop," she repeated and crossed her arms over her chest.

Jon glanced back at Rand, giving him a wild leer, then walked towards his wife. Rand was fuming. *How dare anyone to accuse him of doing that!*

Rand watched his neighbors head into their house and he stared in disbelief. As Jon entered the house, he glanced back at Rand. Both men stood their ground and glared at each other.

Rand stormed into his house seconds later and went right to his office and flung open his desk drawer. The glass tumblers inside rattled and the fifth of vodka flew to the back of the drawer. He grabbed the bottle and a glass and poured as much of the alcohol as would fit in the tumbler.

He drank the entire glass full down in one long swallow. He was irate and could feel his blood pressure rising. He poured another glass of vodka and swallowed this one just as fast.

He began pacing his office and ran his hand through his hair. He recalled the accusation and took the empty glass in his hand and threw it against the wall. The glass shattered and fell to the floor.

He went back to his desk, grabbed another tumbler, and filled it up. As he drank this round of vodka, he felt his anger start to dissipate. He sat in his chair and finished the drink.

He looked at the bottle of Vodka and saw it was almost empty. He got up, grabbed his car keys and headed out to his vehicle. He needed to get to the liquor store for another bottle.

***

As he pulled into the parking lot of the liquor store, Rand noticed a bar across the street. He slipped his keys into his jeans pocket and decided maybe he needed a change of atmosphere when he had a drink.

He strolled into the bar and waited a few seconds for his eyes to adjust to the darkened room. He heard murmurs of other people, some sitting at the bar and tables, and a few guys playing pool. He walked to the end of the bar and slid onto a stool.

He waved his hand at the bartender and asked for vodka on the rocks. The bartender nodded and poured him the drink. He set the glass in front of Rand and tapped his index finger on the Formica bar.

"Pay up first for the first round," he told Rand.

Rand reached into his jacket, took a twenty-dollar bill and set it on the bar. "How many will this buy?"

"Four, but then there's the tip, which that ain't gonna

cover," the bartender sneered.

Rand set a five-dollar bill down on top of the twenty and nodded. The bartender walked away and went to serve another customer. Rand took the glass and as he sipped the cold drink, he watched the other customers behind him in the mirror behind the bar.

The clientele today were mostly men with a few women intermingled here and there. Not that Rand was looking for a woman. That was the last thing he needed right now. He continued drinking his Vodka when one of the women standing in the back corner caught his eye. She was a brunette and was wearing a pair of hip-hugging jeans and a red camisole shirt. She smiled at him and Rand raised his almost empty glass in salute fashion at her.

He signaled to the bartender for another round and in the mirror, watched the lady approach him from behind. She slipped onto the bar stool next to him and held out her hand.

"Hello, my name's Josephine," her voice was as smooth as his drink.

"Rand, nice to meet you," he took her delicate hand in his and shook it. "So, what brings you here?"

She laughed and patted his forearm. "You noticed me."

"No," Rand laughed. "I mean to this bar in general. Not the stool next to me."

"Oh," she laughed again.

Rand took his fresh drink that the bartender placed in front of him and asked Josephine if she'd like a new drink. She nodded and Rand retrieved another twenty-dollar bill and told the bartender to freshen up his new friend's drink.

He and Josephine sat drinking and talking for what seemed like forever. He learned that she was a manager at a local motel and that she had two adult children who lived out of state. She spent her weekends either stopping in for a drink or at home wallowing away and missing her kids.

Rand checked his wallet and saw he only had another

twenty and decided it was time to head home. He still

needed to buy more vodka across the street, so he needed

the cash.

He stood up, said goodbye to Josephine, and began walking

to the exit. Just before he reached the door, a hand reached

out from behind and took his hand. E looked back and saw

Josephine.

"Want to have some fun?" She asked in a sultry voice.

"Who doesn't," he replied with a grin.

"Let's go down the street," Josephine slurred her words. "I

happen to have a key." She held up a motel electronic key.

Rand smiled down at her and opened the door and allowed

her to exit first. They walked down the block and Josephine

guided him to Room 11 and she popped the door open.

They entered the room and before Rand the door shut,

Josephine had her lips on his.

She was removing his jacket as he backed up to the bed.

When the back of his knees hit the edge of the bed,

Josephine pushed him back and he flopped onto the mattress. As he lay there looking up at her, she was removing her red camisole.

Rand's mouth grew dry as he watched her strip. Under her camisole, she wore no bra and her breasts were full and he reached his hands up to cup them. Josephine's soft skin felt luxurious in his hands. Although he wanted to see Josephine completely naked, Rand shut his eyes. He needed this release. It had been too long since he had a relationship with another woman; or any woman, for that matter.

Even before Marie's death, she and Rand hadn't had an intimate relationship for months. He was always too busy with work and his classes, and Marie was always too tired. He assumed most marriages ended up that way. Life got too busy and romance fell wayside.

"Hey, you still with me," Josephine's voice broke into his memories.

"Yeah, I'm still here," Rand opened his eyes as Josephine,

who had rid her body of her jeans and other pieces of clothing, was climbing on top of him. She straddled his hips and leaned down to kiss him.

As their kiss deepened, Josephine began grinding her hips into his. She pulled his polo shirt over his head and started kissing his chest. She moved lower and lower, and when she reached for his pants, she undid the button and lowered the zipper.

He felt her lips skimming over his skin and her hot breath gave him goosebumps. Without realizing it, Rand moaned when her hand slipped inside his pants and took his hard member in her hand. Her fingers circled his throbbing cock as her tongue swirled the head.

"Feels good, doesn't it, baby?" she whispered.

"Oh, God," he groaned and placed his hands behind her head.

Josephine climbed off him and removed his pants and underwear. She crawled over him and settled her hips over his and took his shaft in her hand again and slowly lowered herself onto him. As her moist pussy accepted him, Rand's hips began moving.

With every thrust he gave her, she met his plunge, allowing him deeper inside. She had her hands splayed on his chest and kept bucking on him like a wild animal in heat. Her head lulled back and she began moaning. Rand placed his hands on her hips and every time he pushed into her, he pulled her hips to his groin.

"Oh my God," she shrieked. "You're gonna make me come!"

"Give it to me, Josie," he growled.

Josephine slammed harder onto him. Her nails dug into his chest and began to moan loudly. Rand kept up with every thrust she gave and when he didn't think he could take anymore, he released.

"Oh God," he clenched his teeth together and felt his body shudder as he exploded.

Josephine's body collapsed onto him and after they both

regained their breathing; she slid off him and got out of the

bed. She walked over to the little table and opened her

purse. She took out a pack of cigarettes and looked at Rand.

"Who's Josie?" Josephine asked as she lit a cigarette

standing beside the bed.

"What?" Rand asked and propped up on his elbows.

"You yelled out the name Josie," Josephine answered and

took a long hit off her cigarette. "I don't mind if you give

me a nickname, but honey, you better not be thinking of no

other woman while you're banging me." She blew out a

stream of smoke and went into the bathroom.

Rand watched her disappear and heard the shower turn on.

Did he say Josie's name? While he was having sex with

this woman?

"Oh my God," Rand whispered. *He did!* He remembered

saying Josie's name.

Rand got dressed and left the motel room as quickly as he

could. He ran back to his car in the liquor store parking lot and turned the ignition on. He laid his forehead on the steering wheel and tried to gain his composure.

"What did you just do?" He yelled and slammed his fist into the console between the front seats.

He put his car in gear and pulled out. He drove home in a trance and when he pulled into the driveway, he realized he had forgotten to get more Vodka.

***

Chapter 7

Rand glared at the email on his laptop screen. It was from the college's board of reviews committee and he had been denied tenure. He ran his fingers through his hair and shut his eyes. How could this have happened Why did they deny him?

Opening his eyes, he reread the text of the email. While he did not meet all the requirements right now, he could reapply the next school year. No further explanation. Just that he had been denied.

He reaches over to his nightstand and grabs his tumbler that he had filled with vodka a few moments earlier. He swallows the entire contents in one swallow, then proceeds to refill the glass. He does this a couple more times and stares at his laptop. The email mocked him.

Rand reached over in his bed and picked up the device. He glared at the screen. He hefted it over his head and threw it across the room. It shattered when it hit the wall and fell to the carpeted floor. He brought his glass to his lips and drank the remainder of the alcohol.

"Fuck you people!" he yelled at the broken laptop. "Screw you all!"

***

Rand wakes up on a cold, hard surface. Through his closed

eyes, he can see daylight. The warmth of the sunshine

makes him subconsciously realize it's more than likely past

eight in the morning. He attempts to open his mouth, but it

feels as if glue was holding his tongue to the roof of his

mouth. The acrid taste is strong, and his lips are parched.

He pushes up and opens his eyes to see he had been

sleeping on the floor of his bathroom. He sits for a minute

with his legs stretched out in front of him and gains his

balance. His body is swaying and he places a hand on the

closed toilet seat to gather his wits.

"What the hell," he muttered.

Slowly, he attempts to get up, but loses his balance a few

times and awkwardly shoves his body into a standing

position. He leans on the bathroom counter and splashes

cold water on his face. He grabs a bottle of mouthwash and

took a mouthful. As he's swishing it around, the mint flavor brings his taste buds to life. He glances in the mirror.

The man staring back at him looks tired. Dark circles have formed under his eyes and the gray hair around his temples indicated he's older than he really is. Rand lowers his head, spits out the blue liquid and turns to leave the bathroom. He stumbles out of the bathroom and sees his bed is still made from the day before. He had never made it to bed last night. He staggers into the bedroom, using his dresser as a guide, and goes to the edge of his bed. He flops onto the mattress and turns his head to one side. He's looking out the window as he tries to remember what happened last night.

All he can conjure up is he was mad. Madder than he'd been in quite some time. His eyes travel to a hole in the drywall near his dresser.

"What the hell?" he cursed. He looks down at the floor below the cracked wall and sees his smashed laptop.

"Sonuvabitch!"

His tenure had been denied. The previous night's escapades

had come back to his thoughts like a tidal wave. He would

have to reapply in ten months. He remembered being

furious at the review board and their decision.

He rolled over and pushed up onto his elbows. He had to

get up and go buy a new laptop. Without one, he couldn't

work, grade papers, or do anything work-related.

"Damn it!" he cursed and sat up on the edge of the bed.

"This is not how I wanted to spend my day off."

Rand slips on a pair of loose-fitting jogging pants and a

sweatshirt and heads for the hallway. He'll make a quick

trip to a big box technology store, buy a laptop, and while

he is out, he'll stop at a liquor store and buy more vodka.

He knows he had run out last night before he drifted off to

sleep.

"Amazing how you remember that, but you couldn't

remember breaking your laptop," he muttered.

He stopped in the foyer and slid on his running shoes,

grabbed his car keys, and left the house. He saw Kenzie's

car wasn't in the driveway, which wasn't abnormal for her on the weekends when she stayed out all night at a friend's place. His eyes traveled next door and he saw Josie's compact car was parked in the Devlin's driveway, so he assumed the girls didn't hang out together the night before. He got into his car, started the engine and sat for a moment, gathering his bearings. He needed a minute to set his vision straight and stop his hands from shaking. He decided a visit to the liquor store would be first, then he could continue on his way to buy the laptop.

He turned down the radio, as he was in no mood to hear about all that was wrong in the world. Hell, he could write his own news broadcast about how everything was wrong in his life.

Rand backed out of the driveway and headed to the closest liquor store that he knew of. The sooner he got there and made his purchase, the quicker he could get back to dealing with his life.

***

On Tuesday, Rand knows he needs to go buy his new laptop. He'd fallen behind in his grading and keeping up to date with his colleagues due to not having access at home to his email and the college's system.

Sunday when he drove off with every intention of getting a laptop, he never made it to the technology store. He had stopped at the liquor store, bought a few fifths of vodka and returned home. His head was pounding, and he wasn't fit to go buy the laptop. He needed to get rid of his headache before he could even think about focusing on making the purchase.

Now Rand cursed at himself for never going back out that day, but his head hurt most of the day. By the time he was feeling somewhat normal, it was too late to venture out as the door closed early. He never stopped Monday on his way home from class because he had so much paperwork to catch up and he put off the task again.

But today he needed to stop at the store. He had a late class and could spend a couple of hours looking over the laptop selection before he'd need to be in his classroom.

He heads out to his car and glances over to see Josie getting out of her car. He yells out a hello and waves. She returns the wave and smiles at him.

"Out early today, I see," he says.

"Yeah," she replies. I went to the store and have a few minutes before I need to head off to class, she replied. "Although, to be honest, I have thought about skipping this first class today."

"Why is that?" Rand inquired.

"I don't need to be in attendance, really," she replied.

"Today is just an extra credit day and I'm maintaining perfect attendance to date and have this class aced."

"That's good to hear," he said and thought about inviting

her along with him when he went shopping. Josie was a delight to be around, and perhaps she could offer some advice on which laptop to buy. "Hey, if you're thinking about skipping the class, do you want to go with me? I have to buy a new laptop... mine is old... and I've been wanting to buy a new one."

Josie was silent for a few seconds, then she shrugged her shoulders. "Sure, why not?"

She slammed her car door and walked across the lawn. Rand unlocked the passenger door and she slipped into the front seat.

Rand drove across town and they went into the store. It took much less time than he had figured it would, as Josie was quite the computer geek. She told him he needed so much memory, faster memory speed and a turbo boost. These were all topics. He had no clue what they meant, but he took her word for it. He made the purchase and saw he had over two hours before he needed to be in class, so he offered to buy her breakfast for her assistance. She agreed and said she was famished, so they headed to a little diner near their cul-de-sac.

While eating and chatting about various topics, Rand watched as Josie became animated when discussing her afternoon class; modern music. Her face glowed and her hands were *speaking* as she talked about the history of the cello. She barely stopped for a breath.

Rand had to admit he was enchanted by the way she could carry on a conversation and be so mature. He hardly added much to the chat, because he was so captivated by her beauty.

Had she always been so pretty? Rand thought.

Even though he had known her all of her life, he never really noticed how beautiful she had become in her adulthood. But recently, he had been seeing Josie from an entirely different view. Her eyes had an allure to them. She had developed into a stunning young woman.

In the middle of his thoughts, Josie reached out and placed her hand on his. Rand looked down at her hand covering his and felt a twinge in his groin. He almost pulled his hand out from under hers, but her skin was soft and he liked how it felt on his hand.

"Oh, sorry," she giggled and pulled her hand away. "I didn't mean to offend you."

"No. You didn't," he replied. "I just... wasn't expecting that."

Josie's eyes grew sultry and Rand felt his mouth grow arid. Josie smiled at him, and the twinge grew stronger. So much so that he had to reposition himself on the bench's booth where he sat. He could feel his cock firming up and knew this wasn't the place for such a scene. Josie picked up her chatter again as Rand tried to pray for his hard-on to become flaccid.

His mind ventured to the one-night stand with Josephine and how Rand had called out Josie's name in the heat of passion.

His cock pulsed in his pants.

He recalled how Josie had hugged him weeks ago when he helped her transfer to his class. Her body was so firm and she felt fabulous in his arms.

His cock trembled.

How Josie's voice was so soothing and he could almost imagine her whispering in his ear.

His pants were growing tighter.

Rand lowered his hand under the table and tried to rub himself.

"You okay, Rand?"

"What?" he stammered. *Had she just called him by his first name?* Josie had always referred to him as Mr. Donovan, but hearing his first name escape her lips so naturally made Rand groan inwardly.

"You seem, a little... distracted," she purred with a grin.

"I'm... I'm fine," he stuttered. He glanced at his phone and laid down his napkin. "But I need to be going. My class starts in thirty minutes."

He took out his wallet, tossed some bills on the table and slowly stood up. He'd been relieved to see his pants weren't as tight as they had been moments earlier and he could walk without holding a magazine or book in front of him.

"Oh, okay," Josie replied and joined him.

They walked out to his car in silence and Rand was never so alleviated to have escaped the humility of having a boner when being touched by his daughter's best friend.

After he dropped Josie off at her home, he went to work. His mind drifted to their breakfast and how her touch had affected him so much. His thoughts then went to how she would feel beneath him, naked in bed.

When he pulled into his parking space at the college, he needed a minute for his cock to relax and shrink.

"My God," he exclaimed in his car. "She's going to be the

death of me."

Chapter 8

"Oh my God! Did I just do that?" Josie laughed and danced around her room. "I flirted!" She fell onto her bed and couldn't believe she had followed through with her plan.

For the last week, she had been thinking non-stop about Rand. She had never really noticed just how attractive he was. Sure, he was her best friend's father and she'd known him her entire life, but sometimes you don't see what's right in front of you.

While they were in the car, Josie had fantasized about

kissing Rand, but she couldn't work up the nerve to do it.

She wanted to do that more than anything, just to feel his

lips on hers, and she suspected he was a good kisser.

"Damn it," she sat up on the bed. She had lost her chance

for that kiss when she chickened out. "It's okay. I'll find

another opportunity."

She smiled and got ready for the day. She figured she'd

have many chances in the future for more "hands-on" time

with Rand. She'd make sure of it.

***

"So, this Saturday?" Kenzie asked Josie. "I've missed

hanging out."

"Yeah, me too," Josie said as she shut her laptop.

They were in Josie's room for the last hour, chatting while

Josie finished a few pieces of homework. She had a big

project due at the end of next week, but she was almost

done, so having a girls' night and sleepover was just what

she needed. Especially if the sleepover was at Kenzie's.

This would allow Josie to show Rand how she felt.

"So, sleepover, junk food and movies?" Kenzie clapped her

hands.

"Absolutely!" Josie smiled. "I need some downtime."

"Yeah, you do," Kenzie agreed and fiddled with the fringe

on Josie's comforter. "I've been so busy, and I know you

have too. I think this is just what we need."

"I know it's exactly what I need," Josie stared off, thinking

about the double meaning of her answer.

That day after their shopping excursion and then flirting

with him had her sexual desires all pumped up and she

couldn't stop daydreaming about having Rand ravish her

body. She had so many scenarios she'd played through on

her mind and now, perhaps this coming Saturday, she'd

have the chance to live with one of them.

Her thoughts went to the other night when she pleased

herself while thinking about Rand.

She had locked her bedroom door and lay on her bed. She

shut her eyes and began thinking about Rand touching her.

Josie moved her hand to her breasts and began tweaking

her nipple, all the while imagining it was Rand who was

manipulating it.

Her other hand moved down her stomach and slipped in

between her legs. She rolled her head back and arched her

back as her fingers rubbed her clit. At first, she was gentle

and stroked and swirled her fingers, but when she saw

Rand's face in her mind, her fingers moved quicker.

Before she knew it, Josie was gasping and her hips were

grinding into her fingers. Pleasuring herself had never been

so satisfying. After she came, Josie lay in her bed, trying to

catch her breath.

When her heartbeat slowed down and her breathing was

under control, Josie sat up in bed and grinned. She headed

to the shower with the thoughts of this being another

chance to imagine Rand naked with her.

***

Josie knocked on the front door of the Donovan home.

Normally, she'd just go to the back door and enter the

kitchen without announcing herself, but she thought to play

into her plan to seduce Rand, she would knock on the door

and, knowing he'd be the one to open the door, she could

make her presence known.

When they were at breakfast that day and she flirted with

him, she picked up on his excitement. She saw it in his eyes

first, and she definitely saw his enthusiasm in his groin

when they were in his car. His pants were so tight across

his crotch, she thought his cock would split his pants. If she

had the confidence, she would have reached over and

stroked him.

"Oh, God," she moaned as she waited for Rand to answer the door. She felt her pussy grow moist; which was a daily occurrence lately.

"Hey, Josie," Rand said after he opened the door. "Kenzie is up in her room."

He stepped aside, allowing her inside. She walked in and casually made sure to brush her arm against his abdomen, which sent twinges through her body. She inhaled as she *bumped* into him, and she could smell a woodsy scent.

"Oops, sorry," she mumbled.

"It's okay," he whispered.

She glanced up at Rand and saw a gleam in his eyes. And knew she was causing him to think the thoughts she had been conjuring up. She smiled at him and then walked towards the stairs. She made sure she took the steps slowly, hopefully allowing Rand a good look at her swagger.

When she reached the top of the stairs, she glanced back at him, and sure enough, he was watching her every move.

She smiled again and turned to knock on Kenzie's door.

She entered the room when she heard Kenzie call out to

her.

"Hey, you're early," Kenzie said as she was applying

makeup at her vanity table.

"What's up with the makeup?" Josie asked and set her

overnight bag on the bed. "I thought we were staying in."

"We are," Kenzie replied. "I just felt like putting on

makeup."

"Oh, ok." Josie, who rarely wore makeup, sat on the edge

of the bed and watched her friend change her natural face

into a work of beauty.

"You know what?" Kenzie said as she finished applying

her makeup a few minutes later.

"What?"

"Let me do your makeup."

"What? No," Josie said. Then she stopped. "Well, maybe.

Sure."

"Really?" Kenzie sounded surprised. "You've never agreed to this."

"Well, we're not going out anywhere, so why not?" Josie shrugged her shoulders, thinking how she may be more attractive to Rand if she had makeup on and looked better. After all, Kenzie was practically a pro at applying makeup, and when her best friend had all her makeup done, she was stunning.

Josie took the seat that Kenzie had just vacated and let her best friend work her magic. The entire time Kenzie was putting on the makeup, Josie fantasized about how Rand would react to how she looked. When Kenzie was finished, Josie stared at her reflection in the mirror.

"Holy crap," Josie whispered. "Wow!"

"Yeah, you look gorgeous," Kenzie smiled. "You should consider wearing makeup more often. You look so... different."

"I'll say," Josie turned her head slightly, admiring the work

Kenzie had done.

"I'm gonna go make some popcorn and get some other

snacks," Kenzie walked to her bedroom door. "Wanna

help?"

"Sure," Josie replied, trying to remain calm and not show

her excitement with the hopes of running into Rand while

they were downstairs. She wanted to see his face when he

saw how beautiful she looked.

Ten minutes later, the girls were back in Kenzie's room,

sifting through DVDs and deciding which to watch first.

Josie hid her disappointment at not seeing Rand when they

were in the kitchen. She even took her time picking out

which snack to take back upstairs. It wasn't until Kenzie

got impatient and told Josie to hurry up, as she didn't want

to be down here while her dad was in the house. They still

weren't really speaking, and Kenzie avoided her father at

all costs.

The girls had watched a total of three movies and eaten all

their snacks when Kenzie yawned and declared she was going to bed. Both girls brushed their teeth and climbed into Kenzie's bed. They chatted for a few minutes before Kenzoe yawned and whispered goodnight.

Josie lay in bed, listening to her friend breathe. As soon as Kenzie's breathing became shallow, she knew her friend was asleep. She glanced at the clock on the nightstand and figured she'd give it ten minutes to make sure Kenzie was sound asleep.

The minutes ticked by slowly and Josie was growing impatient. She thought she heard someone walking up the stairs and hoped it was Rand, because if it was, then her plan was going perfectly.

She rolled over to look at the door of Kenzie's room and saw a light flick on from under the door. It was him! Josie's anticipation grew and she felt her stomach flutter.

She looked at the clock again. She had six more minutes before she could leave the bed.

The light flicked off from below the door frame and Josie

saw she only had two more minutes. She listened to

Kenzie's breathing, slow, shallow and steady. She was

definitely asleep.

Josie sat up and slowly moved to the edge of the bed. She

stood up, glanced back at Kenzie, who hadn't moved an

inch, and made her way to the door. Josie quietly opened

the door and exited the bedroom. She tip-toed down the

hallway the short distance to Rand's bedroom. She saw

under the door that there were no lights on in the bedroom.

Carefully, Josie opened the door and entered his room. She

could see his body in the bed thanks to the moonlight that

entered through the windows. She quietly walked to his bed

and pulled back the covers on the opposite side of where he

was sleeping and slipped onto the mattress. She left herself

uncovered and laid down next to Rand.

He moved slightly, but seemed to be in a twilight sleep.

Josie moved closer and put her hand under the blanket and

inched her hand across his abdomen, then lower. Her hand caressed his shorts and she found his cock. While flaccid, it only took a minute of her fingers stroking across the fabric to raise his awareness. When his member began to harden, she slid her hand under his shorts and took his cock in her hand.

He moaned a little and she wrapped her fingers around his shaft and began stroking it. When Rand shifted in his haze of sleep, her hand began massaging him in upward strokes. He moaned again. Using her other hand, she lowered the waistband of his shorts, allowing her more movement.

"Oh, God," he muttered as she felt his cock throb in her grip.

She pushed aside the blanket and carefully, without loosening her grip on him, wiggled out of her shorts. She straddled on top of him and, using her hand, guided his stiff member into her. She sank slowly onto him and felt the pressure of his shaft penetrating her pussy.

She clenched her muscles and he moaned. Once she was settled and had his entire length inside her, Josie began grinding into him.

His hands found her hips and helped guide her motion. They moved in unison and with each thrust of his hips, her body met his movement. Josie was rocking on top of him and laid her hands on his chest for leverage and to help her grind deeper.

"Oh, God, Josie. Yes," he murmured and his hands moved from her hips to under her tee shirt. As he pinched her nipples, Josie lulled her head back and pumped hard on his cock. She could feel it growing inside her and that caused her to moan.

"Yes," he groaned. "Faster," he encouraged her. "You feel so good."

Josie began thrusting harder and faster. She placed her hands on her thighs and bounced on him.

"Yes, yes," she muttered as she felt her pussy vibrate.

"Come, Josie, come now," Rand mumbled.

"Oh, yes," Josie felt her release. She flooded him and felt his shaft erupt, filling her.

Their movements slowed and Josie collapsed onto Rand's chest. His arms wrapped around her and they lay entwined for a few moments. As their breathing slowed, Rand kissed the top of her head as it lay on his chest.

"What was that?" Rand whispered in the dark.

"It's what I wanted," Josie replied. "And I thought you wanted it, too."

"Hmm," he murmured and stroked her back. "Yes, I definitely wanted that... and needed that." He kissed the top of her head again.

Josie slid off Rand's body and laid her hand on his chest while one of her legs crossed over his leg. She lay there for a few seconds and listened to his heartbeat.

"I didn't know," Rand whispered. "I had no idea that you... I had no clue you... Felt like this." she filled in his words. "I didn't either."

"When did you know?"

Josie remained silent, thinking. "I don't know the exact moment, but I would have to say it's been building for a short time now."

Rand groaned. "Please tell me that Kenzie doesn't know."

"No," Josie giggled. "No one knows, but you."

"Does Kenzie know you aren't in the room?"

"I waited until she fell asleep," she whispered.

"You have to go back there," Rand warned.

"I will. Just give me a few more minutes," Josie purred.

'Okay," Rand whispered.

They lay in silence when Rand spoke.

"You weren't a... a virgin, were you?"

Josie kissed his chest, "No. I've had other... boyfriends."

"Good," Rand replied.

They stayed together for another hour. They whispered to each other on occasion, but Josie was just enjoying their time together and how Rand made her feel. The way his fingers caressed her skin and the way hearing his sultry voice made her body tingle.

When she got out of Rand's bed to return to Kenzie's room, Josie leaned down and kissed Rand. He placed his hand on her cheek as their kiss deepened.

As she snuck back to her friend's bedroom, Josie felt so complete. She was smiling and couldn't contain her emotions. As much as she wanted to share this experience with Kenzie, as the two girls often shared their sexual escapades, Josie didn't dare. This relationship needed to remain a secret.

Chapter 9

Josie had never felt so good about her life as she did right now. Her studies were going exceptionally well, her grades put her in the cum laude GPA and her relationship with Rand was progressing every day.

It had been a few weeks since they'd first made love during

123

the sleepover and they had been able to find time for one

another since then. Sometimes it was a long afternoon at a

local motel where they'd lay in each other's arms for hours.

Other times, they would share a 'quickie' while Kenzie was

out of the house, or in between classes at the college. No

matter how they were able to appreciate each other and

share in a few moments of passion, Josie was taking

pleasure in every second.

She'd find herself daydreaming during lectures about

meeting up with Rand. She'd find herself fantasizing about

buying a negligee to surprise him the next time they met at

a motel.

Yes, life was perfect.

She wasn't the only one to notice the change in her attitude

and behavior. Kenzie mentioned it the other day when they

had been sitting outside during a break in between classes.

Colin, the boy who had consoled her months ago about her

scholarship dilemma, had stopped by and sat with the girls

for a few minutes.

Josie had flirted with Colin and when he left, Kenzie had pointed out the provocative behavior. At the time, Josie didn't know she had been playful, but after Kenzie's acknowledgment, Josie laughed. She had been coy with Colin and she had seen him blush a few times while the trio chatted. Kenzie even commented, after Colin had left, that whatever Josie was doing differently to keep it up. She'd finally come out of her shell.

Was it time to come clean and announce their relationship?

Luckily, Kenzie didn't push the issue of what had changed in Josie's life to make her so happy or different. Josie made a mental note to talk with Rand about this.

She had started to imagine them sharing dinners with Kenzie or her parents and revealing their love for one another. In her mind, every scenario played out perfectly and her parents and Kenzie were happy for Rand and her.

Congratulations were shared and it was a typical happily ever-after scene.

Josie had planned on meeting Rand tomorrow for lunch the next day and she would talk with him about it. She didn't feel right about revealing their relationship to anyone without his knowledge or consent.

***

Rand arrived at the bar and restaurant twenty minutes ahead of Josie. He wanted to be here for a few minutes alone, enjoy the quiet time and have a drink. He had had a horrible morning and needed to settle his nerves down. The bar and restaurant, Marcus's, specialized in upscale bar food on their menu and also served alcohol to patrons, beginning at noon. He knew Josie loved the greasy bar food selection, and he appreciated the alcohol being served so early in the day, so this had become their regular meet-up location.

He downed his first drink, then signaled to the server for a

refill. If he was lucky, he could consume both drinks before

Josie showed up. As he waited for his next glass, Rand

thought about how his day had gone from bad to worse in

the blink of an eye.

His TA, teacher's aide, informed him she was leaving

college, and he'd have to find a new assistant; which meant

he'd have to train the new TA quickly. In between

reviewing his old applications from the TA pool, he had

received at the beginning of the semester; he got a text

message from Kenzie stating something was wrong with

her car and that he needed to get it to a mechanic.

He had made an appointment to get her car towed to the

mechanic he used, then as his second class of students

began filing into his lecture room, he got a text from Josie

saying they 'needed to talk' when they met in a few hours.

The 'we need to talk' statement *never* went well. As much

as he wanted to text her back and inquire what was wrong, he saw one of the college tenure review board members walk into the room. He walked over to the man and asked if he needed help.

"No, just here to observe," the man, Ken Gilbert, replied and slipped into one of the seats at the back of the room.

"Great, just what I need," Rand muttered as he went back to his desk.

Too many distractions in such a short amount of time had him opening his bottom desk drawer. He hoped he had a sip or two in his flask because he felt he would be needing it to get through the next two hours.

No such luck. His flask was dry and he didn't have another bottle handy. He had left a full bottle he'd purchased yesterday in his car and he couldn't just leave his students to go retrieve it without raising questions from Ken Gilbert. Rand inhaled deeply and told himself he could get through the next one hundred and twenty minutes without a drink.

He'd have to.

As soon as class was over, Rand made a hasty exit. He didn't care if Ken Gilbert wanted to chat or not. He needed to get to the bar to meet Josie. On the way over, he opened the fifth of vodka he had stashed under the passenger seat and took a few swallows. As the alcohol slid down his throat, Rand felt the pressures of the last couple of hours start to ease away.

He'd had four emails from possible new TA's come in. Kenzie had texted that a tow truck had picked up her car and he thought he did a great job of teaching with Gilbert in the audience. Now all he had to do was see what Josie needed to talk about, and he would consider the day a win. Seconds after he finished his second drink, Josie came rushing into the bar. She spotted him immediately and strode over at a fast pace. Her quick movement caused Rand to go on high alert that something was amiss, and he was instantly apprehensive about their talk.

"Hey," Josie leaned over and kissed Rand before taking her seat next to him at the table. "Sorry I'm late, but I had to fend off Kenzie on the phone. She was going on and on about her car. I told her she could borrow mine tonight and tomorrow as I don't have class plans."

"That's nice of you," Rand replied, wishing he had had time for a third drink before she arrived. He didn't like when they were together and Kenzie's name came up as a topic. He shied away from that because he felt uncomfortable.

"Yeah, that's what friends are for," Josie smiled. She glanced at the plastic-coated menu sitting between the salt and pepper shakers. "Did you order yet?"

"No, I was waiting for you," Rand replied. He raised his hand and signaled to the server.

"What can I get you?" she asked when she got to their table.

"I'll have an order of the Ham Mac 'N Cheese Bites and an

order of the pork belly sliders," Josie said without even looking at the menu. This was her usual lunch order.

"And for you?" the server looked at Rand.

"I'll have the Korean Street Tacos and a side of chips and salsa," he replied.

"Drinks?"

Josie ordered a lemonade and Rand ordered a cola. The server raised an eyebrow, but Rand dismissed the inquiry.

"So," Rand leaned in once the server left. He entwined his fingers together in the shape of a steeple. "What do we need to talk about?"

"Oh, yes," she exclaimed.

Josie began her story from yesterday with her time spent with Kenzie and Colin. She even included how Kenzie had taken notice of her flirting with Colin. Rand listened to her speak and had a feeling of where the conversation was heading, but he didn't want to cut her off. He loved listening to her voice. It was very soothing and helped him not think about ordering another drink.

"So, what do you think?" she asked, her voice full of promise and enthusiasm.

Rand took a second before he responded. He didn't want to burst her bubble, but he needed to be pragmatic about what she was proposing and how he was going to explain how it wasn't a good idea.

"I can understand why you want to share *us* with the world," he began.

"Oh, great, there's a *but* coming," her smile dissolved and her lips turned pouty.

"It's not necessarily bad *but*," Rand replied and reached out to take her hands in his. "I'm just thinking of repercussions that could arise."

"Like what?" she glanced at him.

"Well, for starters," he lowered his voice. "Right now, Kenzie and I aren't exactly on good speaking terms. I'm doubting she'd find joy in knowing I was happy, especially with her best friend."

Josie nodded and bit her lower lip as if she were mulling over that possibility. Rand stroked the back of her hand with one of his fingers. Subconsciously, he was doing this as a way to comfort Josie and the incoming blow of more reasons, as this was not going to happen.

"Okay," Josie replied. "Next reason?"

"Now why are you assuming there's more?" he asked with a grin.

"Because I know you well enough, Rand. You never have just one answer," she returned the smile. "You're a man of many words."

"True, and especially when it comes to such an important matter," he replied, relieved she seemed to be open-minded to discuss the pitfalls of going public with their relationship.

"Okay, what's the second reason?" she quipped as the waitress brought them their drinks.

"Two." He held up one finger, then chuckled and held up a second digit. "I'm a professor and you're a student..."

"Say no more." she held up a hand. "I hadn't considered that."

"Three," he held up a third finger. "I highly doubt your parents would be overly happy with this."

"I don't know," she replied and took a drink of her lemonade. "My parents are pretty open-minded."

"Not *that* open-minded," he smiled. "I'm not sure how I would react if the roles were reversed."

"Oh," Josie frowned.

They sat in silence for a minute and the waitress reappeared, bringing us our food. Josie dug right in and Rand considered excusing himself and going to the restroom, and passing by the waitress and ordering another vodka, but squashed the idea. As long as Rand was with Josie, his need for alcohol seemed to dissipate.

"I see what you're saying," she replied and scrunched up

her nose. "I hadn't considered all the ramifications and how many people our being together could possibly affect."

Josie remained quiet and fiddled with her food. She seemed in deep thought, so he figured he'd let her sort all the information. Rand was halfway finished with his tacos when she spoke.

"Do you think what we're doing..." she stopped and looked around the dark bar.

Rand waited. He didn't want to lead her in her thoughts. He knew she'd come up with the words and express herself. That was one of the deeming qualities he liked so much about her. She didn't act like a typical young person. Kenzie was the perfect example. Rand's daughter would fly off the handle, even after being given all the facts and knowing what could happen.

Josie was beyond her years, in his opinion. Not exactly what people would consider an 'old soul', but she was mature

"Do you think we should take a step back?" She held up her hands again to stop him from talking. "Just so you know, I don't want to. What I want right now is for you to take me to a hotel room and have your way with me." Rand stared at her. He lowered the taco that was halfway up to his mouth and grinned. "I'd like nothing more myself, but let's eat, talk and just enjoy the moment."

Rand knew they'd end up going to a motel and satisfying each other after their lunch. It's how every meal seemed to end with them. But for some reason, he wanted to savor their conversation.

Rand didn't have friends outside of work, and being able to have a serious conversation felt good to him. Sure, they had their pillow talk after making love and ravishing each other, but what they were discussing now was much more important than Rand slamming into a motel room and tossing Josie on the bed, stripping her clothes off, and going down on her.

"Earth to Rand," Josie laughed. "Where were you? You have the biggest smirk on your face."

"Let's go," he tossed down his taco and dug out his wallet. He tossed a few bills on the table and grabbed her hand.

"What? Rand?" She jumped out of the chair.

"I want you now, Josie." he placed his hand behind her neck and pulled her into a kiss. "I want you now... right now."

"Oh," Josie giggled. "Then let's go. I wasn't sure how much longer I could've maintained not jumping you."

Rand drove fast to the motel a few miles away as Josie leaned over, unbuttoned his pants, and undid his zipper. It only took her a few seconds of stroking his shaft for it to become stiff. She lowered her head and wrapped her mouth around the tip while her hand continued stroking.

"Oh, God, Josie," Rand moaned and placed one hand on top of her head, holding it down.

As her hand gripped his cock, her tongue swirled the tip.

Rand strained to keep from coming too soon. His fingers clutched the steering wheel as she lightly skimmed her teeth along his throbbing manhood.

"Oh, Josie," he groaned and slowed down to turn into the motel's parking lot. "You need to stop. We're here."

She raised her head and used a finger to wipe away the moisture from her lips. She smiled at him and then kissed him deeply.

"You better hurry and get the room," she whispered. "I'm feeling extra naughty today."

"Oh, God, you're going to be the death of me," Rand's mouth hungrily took hers. "I'll be right back."

They were inside the room within minutes. Once the door slammed shut, Josie was taking off Rand's clothes. She had removed his jacket, shirt, and pants before he knew it. She began stripping out of her clothes and once she was naked; they fell into bed.

Rand pushed her up so her head was resting on the pillows

and he lowered himself. Once he was positioned between her legs, he began licking and kissing her inner thighs. She placed her hands on his head and arched her back.

Rand spent a few minutes teasing Josie. His fingers would slide across her moist clit and she'd moan and call out his name. Her hips were thrusting into him as her hands held his head close.

"Rand, taste me,' she whimpered. "I can't take much more of this."

"Shh," he whispered in between kissing her thighs and then moving to her mound. His fingers found her wet pussy and he slowly entered her. When her hips were bucking and she had her hands on top of his hand, guiding him to where she felt the most pleasure, Rand lowered his head and began sucking on her. Every so often, his teeth would nibble her wet flesh.

"Now, Rand, now," Josie growled. "I need you inside me."

Without waiting another second, Rand pulled himself up

and settled between her legs. He stared into her eyes as his cock plummeted into her. She moaned, rolled her head back and her hips kept up the motion with him. As they made love, Rand lowered his head and kissed her. Josie greedily accepted his kiss and wrapped her hands around his back.

"Oh, my God, Jose," Rand whispered. "You are so beautiful."

"Mmm," she murmured. "I'm going to come, Rand. Go faster."

Rand's hips moved faster. He lifted her legs and laid them on his shoulders. As he stroked her calves and thrust deep into her, Josie began to pant.

"Oh, yes," she repeated over and over.

"Give it to me," he prodded her orgasm on. "I'm coming, Josie." His pumping became uncontrollable as he released into her.

"Oh, yes!" Josie wailed and grab ahold of Rand's forearms.

"Yes!"

Rand collapsed onto Josie and he could hear her heart beating. He rolled off her and took her in his arms. They lay in the darkened motel room in silence.

Rand never wanted to moment to end. He could imagine waking up every morning with Josie in his arms. Although he wasn't sure it would ever happen. And that was a bittersweet thought.

Chapter 10

Rand stopped at the liquor store on his way home from work and picked up a few fifths of vodka. He'd be spending the weekend at home grading papers and doing midterm grades, and after the week he'd had, Rand knew a

little relaxation and time to unwind was needed.

He got back in his car and drove home. As he pulled into

his driveway, he saw Josie getting out of her car. He waved

to her, and she returned the gesture. When Rand parked his

car and got out of it, he saw Josie's dad, Jon, pulling in

behind Josie. Rand decided to slip one bottle of alcohol into

his laptop bag, and he'd get the other ones later. No sense

in letting the neighbors know how much he had.

Rand walked to his front door and waved to Jon, whose

only response was a quick nod. Rand unlocked the door

and went right to his office. He dropped his bag on the desk

and went back to the door to close it. He peeked out the

door and saw neither Josie nor Jon. His phone dinged in his

pocket, so he dug it out.

Josie had messaged him. She wanted to know if they could

meet later. She was aroused and wanted to be with him. He

told her yes and hat he'd meet her at the diner around the

corner from their normal motel.

Rand went back into his office and set up his laptop. He had a couple of hours to do his work before he'd have to leave to meet Josie. It had been a few days since their last rendezvous and he had to admit he was feeling amorous, too.

Rand set to work and poured himself a drink. He emptied the bottle in his desk drawer and replaced it with the new one in his laptop bag. He sipped his drink and uploaded grades into the college system. He was halfway through with grades when he saw it was time to leave and meet Josie. He emptied his glass in one swallow and grabbed his car keys.

He saw Josie's car still in her driveway when he left the house. He jogged to his car as a light rain had begun.

He drove to the diner and waited for her to arrive. He took his flask out of his jacket pocket and opened it. He took a sip and glanced around the parking lot. Only a few patrons and no one to see him sneaking a drink or two in the middle of the afternoon. He stuck the flask in between the front seats when he saw Josie pull in.

She parked a few spaces over from Rand. She got out of her car and strode over to Rand's. She slipped into the passenger seat and leaned over to give him a kiss.

Rand backed out of the parking space and began driving towards the motel. Josie leaned over and was kissing his neck and rubbing her hand on his groin.

"Mmm," Rand murmured as he drove.

When Josie nibbled on his ear, Rand's hand slipped off the steering wheel and he slammed on the brakes. The car skidded a little on the slick road and Rand shoved Josie back into her seat and attempted to get control of his sedan.

"Oh my God," Josie grabbed hold of the passenger door handle. "Whaat the hell happened?"

Rand steered the car to the side of the road and breathed a sigh of relief. "Must've hit a slick spot."

Josie was holding her hand across her chest and breathing hard from the anxiety of what had just happened.

"That was not cool," Josie said.

"I'm just glad there were no other cars on the road here," Rand agreed.

"What's this?" Josie asked and held up Rand's flask.

"Th-that's nothing," he stammered, and he reached for it, but Josie yanked it out of his reach.

She eyed him suspiciously and unscrewed the cap and smelled it. "Have you been drinking?"

Rand didn't want to lie to Josie, as they had a real open relationship, but he also didn't want her to know he'd been drinking before she arrived.

"Rand?" Josie pushed the inquiry.

"Yeah, Josie," he replied. "I had a sip before you got here."

"What?" she squeaked. "Drinking and driving? That is so *not* cool, Rand."

"Josie, it's not like that," Rand began and ran a hand over

his face. "I've had a very trying week and was just unwinding."

Josie squinted her eyes and glanced at him. She screwed the cap back on the flask and rolled her window down. She tossed the metal container out the window and it clanked on the cement.

"Is this a new thing?" Josie asked as she rolled up her window.

"Josie," Rand sighed. "Don't read too much into this."

"Tell me, Rand. How long have you been drinking to unwind?"

"Josie..." he reached over to take her in his arms.

"No, Rand," she pulled away from him. "Do you realize if another car had been driving down the road, we could have been seriously injured? Do you not see that?"

"Of course, I do," Rand said. "But there wasn't."

"Not this time," Josie cried. "But how many other times have you been driving, with me in the car, and you were drinking? How many Rand!"

"C'mon, Josie, stop it," Rand tried to calm her down.

"Nothing happened."

"Not this time, but what about next time?" She began

ranting.

"Josie, you're making something out of nothing," he

replied.

"Something out of nothing? Really, Rand!" she yelled.

"Don't you remember what happened to Marie?"

"That's uncalled for," Rand yelled back.

"Oh, no! It's definitely called for," she sobbed. "You

could've killed us!"

Rand remained silent. He had no answer. His mind went to

Marie and that night when she had been killed in a car

collision. Granted, the other driver hadn't been drinking or

on drugs. The other driver just lost control of the car he was

driving. Just as Rand had just done.

"You know what? Forget this." She reached over, opened

her door and got out of the car. "I'll walk back to my car and don't follow me. Leave me alone!"

Josie slammed the door and began walking away. Rand watched her until she turned the corner near the diner. He got out of his car, circled it and picked up his flask. As he was going back to the driver's side of the sedan, Josie drove past and shook her head when she spotted the flask in his hand.

Rand cursed and got in his car. He opened the flask, took a drink and threw the container on the passenger side floor. "Damn it," he banged his hand on the steering wheel.

He sat there on the side of the street for a minute, regaining his composure. Nothing had happened. No one got hurt. But was Josie, right? Deep down, Rand knew she was, but he was able to get control of the car. He had been distracted by her touch. This incident had nothing to do with him having a few drinks.

"Technically, it was Josie that did this," Rand muttered and put his car in gear and drove home. He wanted to give Josie a few minutes to get to her home and into her house. Rand took the side streets and drove slowly. H didn't want to see her when he pulled into his driveway.

He'd give her a few days to calm down, then he'd message her. When she'd had a chance to settle down, he'd talk with her and explain. She'd see that he meant no harm. She'd understand that it was a onetime incident.

Rand pulled into his driveway and saw Josie had made it home safely, and he breathed a sigh of relief. He went into his house and immediately went to his office and poured himself another drink. His hands were shaking from the scene with Josie, and after a few minutes when the alcohol entered his system, his nerves calmed down and he felt much better.

Chapter 10

Two weeks later...

Rand sat in his chair, staring at the drawer of his desk. He took the two bottles of vodka out of the drawer and set them on the desktop. He leaned back in his chair and steepled his fingers near his chin.

It was time.

After the scare with Josie almost two weeks ago, Rand took a hard look at his life. Ever since Marie died over a year ago, Rand had been on a downward spiral. He didn't notice it, but wasn't that the way these things happened?

Over the last few days, Rand pinpointed the moment he turned to drinking and how he convinced himself he was a better person and succeeded in getting through all of life's trials and tribulations when he drank.

Looking back now, he realized the grip his drinking had over him. He had almost lost Kenzie, figuratively, not physically. For months, his daughter refused to talk to him. For months, while he and Josie found solace and comfort in each other's arms, he didn't care if Kenzie hated him or not.

Josie had ignored his contact for a few days after the car incident, but eventually, she messaged him, and they talked through the messages. They came to a mutual agreement and understanding that while it had been fun and exciting and made each of them feel more alive; it was time to move on. Neither regretted what happened or how it happened, but both were happy they had kept their relationship a secret.

Rand and Josie could see clearly how detrimental sharing their connection would have been to their families.

Rand took the two vodka bottles to the kitchen and opened one. He stood in front of the sink and hovered the bottle above it. He needed to do this, but his hesitation caused him to pause. He knew he needed to pour the alcohol out and never look back.

Rand watched his handshake. He closed his eyes and took a deep breath. Keeping his eyes shut, he turned his hand and could hear the liquid spilling into the sink. He kept turning his hand until the bottle was upside down and he listened to no more liquor splashing on the stainless-steel sink.

He opened his eyes, set the empty bottle on the counter and grabbed the second one. He proceeded with the same ritual, except this time, he kept his eyes open and watched the Vodka go down the drain.

He tossed both bottles in the garbage can and sighed. He looked out the window over the sink and saw Kenzie sitting in a lounge chair, sunning herself in her bathing suit. Once he cleaned up this mess and tossed out all the tumblers he had used when drinking, perhaps he'd join his daughter out there and chat. It's been a few days since they've had a chance to catch up on each other's lives.

He returned to his office, grabbed the three glass tumblers he always drank out of, and took them into the kitchen to throw away. He didn't want them in the house as they would remind him of drinking. He dropped them in the trash can and heard the glass break.

"Okay, Randall Donovan, it's a new day," he muttered. He walked to the back door and headed outside to sit next to Kenzie. Rand's attention was drawn to the Devlin's backyard next door as they talked. He heard Josie laughing and saw her sitting on the edge of their inground pool, chatting with Colin, the young man she'd found support in him quite a few times over the last few months. She had issues with her scholarship before she came to Rand for help.

Rand knew the boy from work, and Rand approved of Josie and him starting a relationship, not that Rand's consent. He watched as the young couple talked and laughed every few moments. Seeing how happy Josie was right now made him glad.

Josie had found someone to like and that she could share with her parents without repercussions.

"Dad," Kenzie's voice broke into his thoughts.

"Yes," he replied and looked away from Josie and Colin.

"We should have a BBQ," Kenzie said, and sat up more in the lounge. "We can invite Josie, Colin, and her parents. Like a beginning of summer kick-off."

"That sounds..." He hesitated. "Like a lot of work."

"I'll handle all the details," Kenzie giggled. "You just need to man the grill."

"Okay," Rand said and glanced back at Josie.

While he missed his time and lovemaking with Josie, he

knew this was for the best.

After they had talked, he felt at ease knowing they were making the right decision. They still messaged each other about topics that interested them both. They had a good relationship that he knew most adults have, and it felt right. Rand would forever be grateful for his connection with Josie. Her appearance in his life in a more personal way came just when he needed it, without him knowing he needed it. He hoped somehow; he had been called into her life for a reason and he had been able to fill the void she required at the time.

Sure, there had been awkward moments in the last two weeks, but Josie handled them quite well for a girl her age. Rand felt tense the first time she came over to see Kenzie, but with her smile, and the way she cocked her head at him, Rand loosened up and settled into a comfort zone.

Josie glanced over, made eye contact with Rand and she smiled. It was as if she knew Rand was thinking about her.

Josie waved and Rand returned the gesture. Colin turned to see who his girlfriend was waving to, and Colin raised his hand and nodded his head in Rand's direction.

Rand nodded at Colin.

"I'm so happy for Josie," Kenzie said.

"Yeah, me too," Rand whispered.

www.ingramcontent.com/pod-product-compliance
Lightning Source LLC
Chambersburg PA
CBHW022130170626
46808CB00002B/930